MERCHANTS AND MAJI.

Also in the Dissolutionverse by William C. Tracy

Tuning the Symphony

To my Favorite nephew

163

MERCHANTS AND MAJI

TWO TALES OF THE DISSOLUTIONVERSE

William C. Tracy

William C3

Space Wizard Science Fantasy

Raleigh, NC

Space Wizard Science Fantasy
Raleigh, NC
www.spacewizardsciencefantasy.com

Publisher's Note: This is a work of fiction. Names, characters, places, and incidents are a product of the author's imagination. Locales and public names are sometimes used for atmospheric purposes. Any resemblance to actual people, living or dead, or to businesses, companies, events, institutions, or locales is completely coincidental.

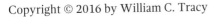

Cover art by Micah Epstein
Interior illustrations by Adam Riong
Book Layout © 2015 BookDesignTemplates.com

Merchants and Maji/William C. Tracy.-- 1st ed.
Library of Congress Control Number: 2016911809
ISBN 978-0-9972994-2-7

Author's website: www.williamctracy.com

For Heather:
For putting up with all this mess.

CONTENTS

Last Delivery

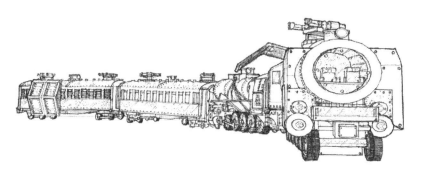

PART ONE

Plots and Deals

- In recent cycles, some merchants have cried foul against the maji raising prices on portal creation. While the portals are the only way to link our homeworlds together, they are also a drain on the already overworked houses of the maji. But I feel passing this cost on may have a worse result. By driving away the traveling merchants who connect our different cultures, I believe we may generate much more contention and even war among the ten species that make up our coalition of worlds.

From a travelogue of Morvu Francita Januti, Etanela explorer and big game hunter

From the safety of my metal transport, I eyed the natives around the market's foreign district. The group of Sureriaj was bigger than it had been five minutes ago, and some of them were holding signs. Others were holding sticks.

"We need to go," I told Amra.

She handed local coinage in change over the table to the gangly Sureri buying spices. "Why? Go where?"

In answer, I pointed one finger to my left, aimed at the growing mob of aliens through the windshield of the transport we used to carry and sell goods. Our market table was set up in the pilot section of the transport, looking out through the open side hatch.

"I don't think they're here to buy our marshfern seed, Prot," Amra said. She moved a protective hand over the colorful piles displayed for maximum scent and visual effect. Past the table and through the hatch, I could see other market-goers perking up at the disruption.

"Maybe they want the *Ibora labat*," I suggested. "It was the best deal on the Lobath homeworld at the time."

"The dried crushed redcap has been selling better," Amra said, but she was already standing, dusting off her yellow wrap.

I let our joke pull the edges of my mouth up, trying not to let her know how concerned I was. I had seen things like this before, and they could get ugly, fast. "Get this packed up. I'm going to get the others moving."

My accountant, and the love of my life, pulled her wrap close to shift her chair out of the way, face tightening. She scraped spare change into a pouch, then reached for the cover to the spice boxes, economical of motion.

I slipped around the edge of the table and down to the ground, calling for my bodyguards and mechanic. "Kamuli! Bhon! Saart! Time to get moving." I waited for a response, shivering in the chilled air. In addition to the growing throng in the market, other Sureriaj wandered through their cold and faded port town like hairy long-legged gargoyles. So many of them in one place had me on edge, though it *was* their homeworld. I could vaguely hear the crowd abusing a Kirian merchant farther down the line of stalls. Her feathery crest was flattened in fear.

No one answered. I pulled myself up into the engine section of the low domed transport, waving away the stink of burning coal. "Saart—what are you doing? We've got a group of Sureriaj ready to—"

"Where's the fire?" rumbled a deep voice. A hairy shape loomed in the corridor. Mogflaratan Saart, Maker, held a massive wrench in one three-fingered paw, pushing up his glasses with the other. There were grease stains in his graying fur and on the belts of pouches across his belly. Working on one of the turrets again. His pet project.

"The fire might be us, in a few more minutes." I told the Festuour. "There's a mob of locals out there who don't look like they want to do business."

Saart wrinkled his long snout, blue eyes peering at me. "I thought the Naiyul port was neutral territory for the families? Won't the constabulary thugs take care of it?"

"I don't want to chance it." I ducked my head back out the door. The mob was chanting something now, with feeling. "Get this thing moving instead of arguing." Saart hrumphed at me, but turned awkwardly in the narrow corridor, grumbling back to the engine.

"Who's arguing?" came another voice. The other Festuour member of my team rounded a nearby building, her mate in tow. "And why aren't I part of it?"

"You and Kamuli get the chocks out from the wheels," I told her. "And keep your handcannons ready." I pointed at the crowd of Sureriaj again. One sign was close enough for me to make out a word in their spidery script: 'go.' I didn't need to be able to read the rest of it.

Bhon grinned up at me with pointy teeth, excited at any prospect of violence. "You got it, boss. We saw them a few minutes ago. We were coming to tell you all, but maybe we can pick off a few on the way out." She sprinted toward the third and fourth sections of the transport—the living and cargo sections—on stumpy furry feet. Kamuli was right behind her, brilliant white teeth and headwrap flashing against her dark skin.

I clambered back to the pilot section, all four sections of the transport rumbling as the engine clanked to life. Amra had the spices back in their boxes, and was clutching the money purse and her ledger where she kept all our expenses. No time to pack this inventory with the rest in the cargo section.

"Everyone ready?" I called into the speaking tubes placed around the pilot's chair. Amra closed the side hatch with a clang, the table and chairs thrust hurriedly out of the way. She climbed into the co-pilot's chair.

"Engine's running," came Saart's voice, tinny, from the speaker.

"Bhon and I are set," Kamuli said from the living quarters.

"Ready," said Amra, jotting down numbers in her ledger, no doubt calculating our losses from closing up early today. She curled a strand of dark hair behind one ear. We had been here less than a week, but I already knew we needed to get off Sureri and to a homeworld less detrimental to our health.

I pushed on one of many levers before me, and the transport crept forward. It was slow to start, but once it got moving, it was hard to stop. The mob blocked the exit to the market road, and there was no way I could turn the transport around without taking half of the sun-bleached buildings with us. More merchant stalls blocked the other end of the road, and my transport didn't do reverse well. I'd rather run into the wall of inhospitable Sureriaj than my fellow merchants, who were packing in a hurry at the rising discontent.

Amra tensed as I made my decision and accelerated. "We'll have to go through them. Hang on!" I yelled into the speakers, and pushed the lever farther. The transport sped up. Several of the mob were pointing now, and I could just make out a couple words of their language filtering through the metal sides of the transport, mostly things like "thief" and "go."

I gritted my teeth and kept moving forward, faster than a walk, not quite fast enough that the group couldn't get out of my way. I didn't want to hurt anyone, especially merchants. Even the liberal families would be quick to revoke our merchant license if that happened. But if an offworlder got injured on Sureriaj? Well, that was their fault.

The transport pressed into the mob now, and several of them banged on the sides. I tried to ignore the metallic pounding.

Then something hit the windshield with a thump. Amra cried out and ducked, and I jerked in my chair. A leafy vegetable of some sort rolled away.

"Boss," came Bhon's voice through the speaker. "These gargoyles are gettin' fresh with the sides of the transport. Want me to pick a few off?"

"No!" I shouted, and ducked again as another rotten vegetable squished into the glass. Amra shook her fist at the offending alien.

"What did we do to you?" she shouted. Then to me, "Why are they all so pale?"

I looked through bat-like faces as I drove. "I think they're all from one of the northern families. Roftun, or perhaps the Baldek family." Both were conservative and isolationist, even for Sureriaj.

"Shove them away if they get too close," I shouted into the speaker, a death grip on the motive lever. I heard the clang of a hatch opening. "No killing!" I hoped Kamuli would rein her fiery mate in, though the large woman held her own share of knives along with her medical pouch. She was as skilled in taking people apart as putting them back together.

The mob crowded close, pushing back as much as the transport pushed them. I heard the engine whine as the mass of people slowed the wheels. I moved the motive lever farther up, giving it more juice.

There was a shout and a clang from outside, and Amra jumped as a curse shot through the speaker system.

"Was that Kamuli?" she asked, and I grunted agreement. The composed woman spoke little and swore almost never.

"Everything alright back there?" I called. I tried to ignore the hostile faces pressed against the windshield.

"Kamuli got hit with a rock!" Bhon growled. "I'm gonna kill those—"

"No!" Amra and I shouted in unison.

"Kamuli?" I asked. If the big woman was down, her mate would go ballistic.

"I am well," Kamuli said through the speaker, though she sounded shaken. "Only bruised."

"We've got to clear a path," Amra said, getting up from her chair. "They're going to stop the transport before we get through, and Bhon won't last that long without shooting one of them." Her dark eyes cast around for objects in the pilot's section. There weren't many. I tried to concentrate on not crushing any angry Sureriaj.

"Aha!" I heard Amra shift something behind the merchandise table.

"What—" I looked around in time to see a spice tray pass by at head height. Fine particles of the orange spice floated through a beam of bright sunlight. My mouth screwed up and directed a fantastic sneeze into my shoulder.

"This should work fine," Amra said. She jerked the

hatch open and flung the stuff out into the crowd.

The reaction was immediate. Sureriaj grabbed at their eyes and mouths, and the pressure on the transport lessened. I pushed the motive lever forward, blinking through tear-filled eyes.

The heavy steel transport was originally made for much bloodier pursuits, and drove through the sneezing and crying Sureriaj with ease. When the last of the four linked sections—our space for cargo—was clear of the mob, I put the transport to full speed, its small wheels churning, leaving the crowd far behind.

"Anyone following?" I asked Amra a few moments later.

She got up again, balancing against the rough roads, and opened the side hatch to peer out. "There's a couple running after us, but they're slowing down. The rest are going after that group of Methiemum who were selling two kiosks down."

I let out a long breath, blinking the last of the spice away. She would have chosen the *Ibora labat*. That stuff was potent. "I don't envy them." I slowed enough to make a wide turn and Amra clung to her seat to keep from falling. Once down a few more side streets, I stopped the transport completely.

"Everyone up front," I called.

We clumped together outside the pilot section. The four parts of the transport were linked together with large coupling rods and pins, but that meant the only way to travel between them was by going outside. Perhaps a flaw of the original designers.

"What the hell was all that about?" said Bhon. Younger than Saart, our other resident Festuour, Bhon was short, covered in light green-yellow hair, and had a snout full of teeth and bright blue eyes. She was also deadly with a handcannon or a crossbow—both hung from the bandoliers crossing her chest—which lent a lot of weight to her words. Or at least a lot of violence. I was glad none of the mob of Sureri had gotten the wrong end of one of her guns, or I would be dealing with a lot more than a shaken crew. Right now, she was dabbing tenderly at a shallow cut on her mate's forehead.

"It was one of the conservative families—Roftun or Baldeks," I said, "though I have no idea why. The Naiyuls are going to be livid they interfered in their trading port affairs."

Sureri was run by the major families of the Sureriaj, each as large as one of the ruling nations on Methiem. The Sureriaj took families seriously. With two males and one female to conceive a child, and with a slow rate of reproduction, the family was the most important social unit to a Sureri. Neither rewards, nor work, nor money, nor love would make a Sureri abandon or betray their family. For the most part.

That was where the disgraced family came in—the Naiyul. It consisted of those Sureriaj from all families, large and small, who had been disowned for crimes and indiscretions. They made a small family all of their own, and ran the one trading port—Naiyul Montufal Desretre—where aliens were tolerated, barely, and bargained with.

"The city is dangerous enough already," Kamuli said. She brushed Bhon away, though with an appreciative smile for her mate. Unmodified by the speaking tube, Kamuli's voice was rich, with thoroughly pronounced vowels. "Should not the gangs in charge be ready to protect their sections of the port?"

There was a thin line the criminal clans toed, as none of the Sureriaj liked outsiders, but it was also the one place on their planet where goods could arrive from offworld. So merchants, if not welcomed, were at least not attacked and robbed on sight. Until today.

"They'll be ready next time," Bhon said, cracking her knuckles. "And there's gonna be turf wars in the next few days over this." Her grin was malicious, and her mate slapped the Festuour's shoulder with the back of her hand.

"Behave."

"Our sales will be terrible until this dies down," Amra said. She looked down at her ledger like a favorite pet. "We might as well throw the rest of the spices in the gutter, except we haven't made enough to buy passage off this world yet." Her skin and dark brown hair had respectively tanned and bleached in the brutal sun that favored the Sureriaj homeworld. The trading town was dry and dusty, and one would think the blazing rays would at least take the time to heat the ground on the way to burning our skin. No such luck. It froze during the night and was merely cold during the day. I was told it was the height of summer.

Saart had been watching the whole exchange, arms crossed, a wrench grasped in one paw. "At least if we dump them, my food won't taste like greenwort mushrooms anymore." He looked between us, then down at Amra's ledger. "If I have to make another flapjack reeking of a squidhead's foot, I may stop cooking altogether. But if we can't sell them, won't that eat into our money like a rat in a seedbag? How much do we have left?"

"I, too, would be interested in seeing return for our hard work with the Lobath," Kamuli spoke up, adjusting her headscarf away from her wound.

"Yeah, we were on Loba for four months to gather this stuff! The transport still stinks of those squiddies."

Bhon looked affronted, though that was similar to her usual expression.

I looked between the two. Kamuli Balion and Shrimasharimsa Bhon, Guarder. They couldn't have been happy on Sureri, where they had to hide their attachment from the xenophobic locals, but they were right that we needed to sell our cargo to leave.

"I know." I spread my hands out, palms up. "These are the best tasting spices we've found in many cycles."

"It didn't help the mushroom farmers of Sa'Lob had very little appreciation of our finer trinkets." Amra put in. "We barely made enough to schedule a portal here."

"To this washed-out excuse for a town," Saart said.

"What can I say? Sureriaj love Lobath spices." I shrugged. Still, I had hoped to make a quick sale and be off to a friendlier homeworld before now.

"The market will be a ghost town for weeks," Kamuli added helpfully.

I ran a hand down my face, and answered Saart's original question. "Like Amra says, we won't have enough for a portal without selling the rest of this." I waved a hand at the cargo section, farther down the road. After several unprofitable ventures, we were living from trade to trade. We hadn't been back to Methiem, where Amra and I hailed from, in almost a full cycle. "Bloody maji, hiking up fees on their portals."

"You can't blame them for everything. Let's pack up for today and find a safe spot to park the transport overnight," Amra suggested.

I nodded. "I'll see if I can run down any good deals tomorrow morning."

"And we'll sell these spices like they're grown from the Nether crystal itself," Bhon said.

* * *

The next morning, back at the market, I sat with Amra, leafing through my notes on merchant contracts. Some dated back all the way to when Saart and I started the business together, many cycles ago. We could have been mercenaries, except the strange fellow we bought the transport from insisted any ordnance was gone, any stored energy dissipated. Saart's pet turrets might have been useful yesterday. I wondered how much mercenaries made.

There had to be someone else on Sureri who wanted to take a transport full of spices.

Wearing a rich wrap the color of the crushed redcap, Amra presided over the trays of fragrant powders displayed like so much colored sand, but we had made only one sale so far.

I flung the sheets down. "There's nothing here. All the smart merchants *know* to avoid Sureri. If I had listened to you the last time we made a big sale, we could be sitting in a little shop on Methiem right now, waiting for the customers to come to us."

"You didn't know the frost radish market was going to tank so soon. Besides, you like traveling in this old thing." She patted a metallic wall companionably.

"But you don't."

"I love you, and that's enough. I just—" She cut off and I sighed.

"I won't subject a child to this life. There's time for that when we're settled."

"You're always set on children. What about time for an actual marriage, and a shop, and the money to keep it running? Kamuli and Bhon make a life together, even traveling with us." She was warming up to the old argument.

I did want children, even if Amra wasn't sure. And while I loved my transport, I didn't want to raise a family in it. "We'll get off this world," I said, "and the next time we hit a good deal, we can sell the transport and open a shop on Methiem rather than sitting in a cold and dusty market stall on another homeworld." I gestured to the deserted market, our only prospective customers a trio of Sureriaj beggars huddled in thin blankets. The two males had lost their mate somehow, but they sheltered a thin child beside them, trying to keep her warm.

Besides our stall, there was one run by two balding Etanela, both half again my height, and one with a lone Kirian woman, crest ruffled and wrinkled arms and legs bare even in the cold. Was she the same one the mob yelled at the day before? She must be even more desperate than us.

"And how long until that deal comes along, Prot?" Amra asked, pulling my attention back. "We've been together six cycles."

I searched for an answer, but was fortunately distracted by a Sureri in a top hat walking purposefully our way, tailored leather coat and tails swishing around wool breeches. He didn't even spare a glance for the other merchants. Bhon materialized from somewhere, hand on one of her holsters, and I caught a glimpse of Kamuli's tall frame through the windscreen, taking in the newcomer's clothes.

"I am thinking yer and yer crew are ready to depart our fine world soonish?" he said in a passable version of the Trader's Tongue. Like all Sureriaj, his legs were longer than mine, his torso shorter, though he was of a height with me. Despite a smaller chest, his arms dangled longer than my own.

"After what happened yesterday? You bet we are."

Amra scowled at the well-dressed Sureri and I laid a hand on her leg beneath the table. My accountant was an excellent records keeper, and kept our enterprise afloat, but she had no sense for a good deal.

But he only bobbed his hairy bat-like head in her direction. His hat cast a shadow in the morning sun, enough to obscure his eyes. "Yer mate, I assume? I wish yer family great bounty. Eyah, yesterday's events were...unfortunate-like. Some of our people are a little excitable with aliens forcin' their way into our world, sellin' foreign wares we donna need." His accent became thicker, and his lip curled up for a moment. Then he smiled, and Amra sat back at the sight. Sureriaj were not pretty to begin with.

"Are you looking for spices?" I asked, directing his attention to our table. And off Amra.

The Sureri opened a hand, palm out. "Nay, but I do have an opportunity for yer."

My eyes rose back to him. "I'm listening."

"If yer will come with me a shortish way, and speak with me grand-dame, I think we can benefit each other greatly."

My eyebrows shot up, despite myself. A grand-dame? It was rare to see Suereri women, given they were outnumbered by the males two to one, though they ran most of the businesses behind closed doors.

"I'll be happy to accompany you," I said. I very carefully didn't leap over the table before he changed his mind. "Let me get one of my guards and we'll be—"

"Just yer self, I am afraid," the gentleman Sureri said, with another of his frightening grins.

I paused, taking into account Bhon, Kamuli, and Amra. Saart was tinkering somewhere. Amra was staring at the alien in disbelief, and I could tell she was about to protest.

"That will be...acceptable," I said quickly, and held Amra's eyes with mine until she closed her mouth, frowning. "My crew will continue to sell our wares here." I crooked a finger for Kamuli to come sit with Amra. The tall woman was the second best negotiator, next to myself.

"Be careful. I don't like this man," Amra whispered. She got up as I did, making for the pouch holding small change. "But I can at least make myself useful and give those beggars some money. Their child looks half frozen."

* * *

The Sureri gentleman led me out of the foreign market and around the first corner. They must have rented out one of the unused buildings.

Though the outside was gray like the rest of the town, once through the front door, the décor changed dramatically. There were fine carpets and tapestries from Festuour, sculptures and paintings from Kiria and Etan, and an immense chandelier, which unless I missed my guess, was studded with precious gems mined on Loba.

Lighted by the fixture was an ancient female Sureri, with several males and a few females surrounding her—certainly all children, nieces, and nephews. She was clothed in a voluminous orange silk dress, overflowing the padded chair she sat in. Her thin white hair had been teased and piled into an enormous pouf larger than her head, hung with feathers and a silky net. Unfortunately, her attire did nothing to reduce the ghastliness of face. The female Sureriaj were just as ugly as the males.

"Sit down, Prot," the grand-dame said. She had done her homework. She pointed with a gloved hand to a small chair on her right and I obediently sat, followed by the gentleman Sureri. This was no small scion sub-family, but surely very close to the main family line—whichever family that was.

"I have heard yer crew is one of the best around to carry cargo in a quick-like fashion." Her accent was light.

"It is that, ma'am," I replied. I tried to judge their lineage from the selection of aliens in the room. They all had similar features, delicate, with pale hair, though I couldn't tell how much was cosmetics and how much was natural. Sureriaj were funny about giving out their names, especially to offworlders, and it was considered rude to ask. They of course knew their own families by sight.

"That is good. Eyah, we know yer must be wantin' to leave our fair homeworld. We have an urgent delivery for Methiem. Would yer be willing to take it?"

I tried to make my expression accommodating, but firm. "If the price is right."

The grand-dame named a sum.

"Ahh...that would...do nicely," I said, trying to keep my jaw from the floor. I wasn't going to get another chance like this, not in twenty cycles of trading. "May I ask what the cargo is, and where it will be received?"

"Nothing illegal, or harmful, if that is what yer imaginin'. Have yer not heard of the epidemic o' the Shudders invading yer own homeworld?" the grand-dame asked. I shook my head. "Eyah, the Methiemum government pays us well for medicine for those sufferin'. It is quite desperately needed. Within the next twenty hours." She made a small gesture and the gentleman stepped forward, giving me a paper with a set of directions.

"This is the location of our warehouse here, as well as the one yer will take the medicine to on Methiem, near Kashidur City." The gentleman handed me a contract, which I scanned. Standard boilerplate, the party of the first part and so on. I read it to the end. The Frente family. I tried to remember my history lessons. They were a fairly liberal family, if I remembered correctly, which may have been why they were helping us escape the recent protests. They couldn't have been happy with the interference in offworld trading.

Someone produced a quill and ink from somewhere, but I hesitated. "I hate to be a bother," I started, but the grand-dame smiled slightly, motioning for me to continue. "I still have a transport full of spices to sell, and I will need something up front to pay for an expedited portal to Methiem."

"Eyah, we happen to have a family feast day comin' up soon. The spices will be perfect like," the grand-dame said. "Yer may sell them at the following location." She nodded to the gentleman, who took my set of directions back and scribbled words barely legible at the bottom. "As to yer fee, yer may negotiate with me relatives at the warehouse. I'm sure they will accommodate yer." The grand-dame folded gloved hands and sat back lightly. It was obvious my chance for questions was at an end.

I looked down. If I didn't sign this contract now, another group would get it within the hour, and this was a sure way to get off this planet. Normally the entire crew made the decision on what to trade. Normally Amra was with me, writing in her ledger and figuring out the plusses and minuses. But this was a good deal—a great bargain, really. One of a kind.

I signed the paper.

* * *

Amra's eyes narrowed, one hand tightening on her ledger. "I'm sure you didn't seal the contract without the approval of the rest of the crew, did you?" The other three crewmembers stood in a circle around us.

"There was no time," I told her, trying to keep my voice level. "By the time I got your nod it would have been gone. And we've got to pick up the new cargo and take it to Methiem in a standard Sureri day."

"Impossible. Scheduling the portal off-world will take longer than that. The one contract can't pay for everything." Amra raised an eyebrow at me.

I showed her the contract, and both eyes went wide. Bhon craned her neck to see.

I could see Amra calculating. "With the profit from this, we could start saving enough to look at places near Kashidur City—"

"Later," I said, though she was probably right. "For now we need to get moving."

"And what about all these spices?" Saart asked. He pushed his glasses farther up his snout. The older Festuour hated wasting anything that might be used in food or repairs. Privately, I agreed with him, but the Sureriaj were not known for their patience, especially with aliens.

"We'll have to sell them at-cost, most likely."

There was a collective groan. Kamuli showed her teeth in something that definitely wasn't a smile.

"I already have a buyer. We'll just have to—" I swallowed, "—let Kamuli sell these off while I negotiate at the pickup site." I didn't look at Amra. If I had let my love run our little shop-on-wheels, we wouldn't have sold enough to get off Methiem in the first place, let alone travel through the ten homeworlds. She would have ended up giving half our profits to needy families. I wasn't uncharitable, but I wanted to support myself before I supported others.

"Can we all agree to follow through with this? We have to move fast, and don't have time for bickering."

Now I did watch Amra. Her eyes were down, focused on her ledger. Reluctantly, she nodded. I looked at the others. Saart had folded his furry arms, tapping his wrench on his shoulder. He shrugged. Bhon rolled her blue eyes, bouncing one of her handcannons off the other paw. She didn't care where we went, as long as she got to shoot something every once in a while. Kamuli looked dubious, but then turned to regard the marketplace. I saw her glance to the merchants not of this homeworld. She wasn't even able to walk hand in hand with her mate. Conservatives like the Sureriaj still frowned on cross-species attachments. She looked back at me, her eyes hard.

I stood, and picked up my stool. "It's settled." As if I hadn't already signed a contract in front of several well-dressed, possibly royal, Sureriaj. "Let's get this place packed up. We have to be at the warehouse as soon as possible."

Packing consisted of breaking down the table, stowing the chairs, and repacking the spices. Saart began stoking the coal furnace that powered the transport, and Kamuli and Bhon shuttered the windows and removed the wheel chocks.

We would have to split the transport for this endeavor, with Kamuli and Bhon driving the living section, which had its own small turbine, towing the cargo section. Saart, Amra, and I would travel in the pilot and engine sections, negotiate the contract, then wait for the empty cargo section at the warehouse.

I passed Amra in the hallway, doing the little dance we all adopted to move around each other in the long, narrow transport sections. She still looked pained, and I knew what she wanted. She was a fabulous accountant, but a lousy negotiator. On the other hand, I had a good sense of market values, but when they were written down, they always got the best of me. That was why we made a good team.

"I could try..." she began as we moved around each other, my hands on her hips, hers on my arms. Her red wrap swirled around my feet.

"No." I wasn't going to be swayed again.

"Come on," she wheedled, "you never let me sell anything off the transport. I can bring in revenue on the spices, no matter how small."

"That's because you don't turn a profit," I told her. "I love you dearly, but you can sell water to a dying man and lose on the deal."

Her mouth turned down in a pretty pout. We were blocking the hallway, but the others were busy. "Let me try, once more," she pleaded. "There's a captive audience. I can sell the spices." Her tone was reaching that certain harmonic that made my eye twitch. Amra could be very stubborn when she wanted.

"Come on, boss, let the gal do it." The voice floated through the metal siding of the transport. Bhon could hear us through the wall. "You can sell quickly, can't you Amra?" she said.

I hesitated, and Amra moved in for the kill.

"Please?" She smiled at me in a way that hinted at brain-melting rewards in the future if I let her have her way.

Mentally noting how my future self owed me, I threw up my hands. "Fine. We're going to lose on them one way or the other. Take the cargo section, but sell the spices as fast as you can. Kamuli can ride with me while I drive the rest of the transport to the meeting place." I gave her the directions the gentleman Sureri had written down.

"I'll find you soon," Amra promised, scooting past me.

"Take Bhon with you," I called after her. "She can at least threaten to shoot someone if they won't buy anything."

* * *

In the pilot's seat, I rumbled along the too-narrow alleys of the market port of Naiyul Montufal Desretre. It probably wasn't the real name, just what the Sureriaj told aliens. Saart was busy keeping the steam engines running smoothly in the next section, and Kamuli stood behind me, watching the bland and windblasted buildings flow by.

Amra headed off with Bhon some minutes before we started out. Both halves of the transport were traveling to the section of the city belonging to the Frente family. The Naiyul ruled the trading town, the only commercial entrance to their planet. Within the city of the disgraced, all but the most conservative of the upright families owned sections, acting like trading embassies.

Kamuli must have wandered down the same line of thought. "Remind me," she said slowly, her words even more precise than usual, "why we decided to travel to the most xenophobic of the ten homeworlds? Who thought this would be a good deal?"

"You know full well who thought it was a good deal," I answered. "This is the only place we could get enough from those spices to buy a portal to the next homeworld."

"The ones we are dumping for whatever Amra thinks is a good price."

I ground my teeth, ratcheting back one of the steering levers. The transport skidded on its wheels to the right, narrowly missing a Sureri mounted on lizardback, trailing a cart filled with red leafy vegetables. He yelled something at us and I waved back cheerily, purposely misinterpreting his intent. Amra had the cargo and living sections, so I had to be careful not to oversteer and ram the engine into any more buildings. There were not many people out today, likely because of yesterday's disturbance. I could move faster through the streets than normal.

"I had not heard of this epidemic," Kamuli said, gripping a handle to keep her balance. "We have been absent from Methiem too long, especially if it is so bad the authorities must import medicine from Sureri." Kamuli kept tabs on local medical news, but since we had arrived here from an isolated community on Loba, her information was dated.

"The Sureri have good medicine," I said. "And the contract insisted the cargo is expected on Methiem by tomorrow morning. It must be an emergency." I swerved again, taking a hard left. I was pretty sure this was the correct turn. The buildings here all looked the same.

A tinny voice emerged from the speaking tube next to my chair. The words were obviously shouted, but came out muffled. "We have an official following us, riding one of those tall beasts!"

"Just what we need!" I shouted back into the tube. "I'm speeding up. Keep the furnace going." Even if they couldn't kill all the aliens that came to their planet, didn't mean they wouldn't try to arrest them on the merest offense. The protest had everyone on edge. I was probably driving too fast, or they were upset about the building I might have nicked a few turns back. I ratcheted the speed lever up another notch.

"Fortunate then that you were contacted to fulfill this contract." The big woman took up her previous line of questioning without a break. Kamuli would never directly confront me. She just poked and prodded. I still wasn't sure how she and Bhon got along without killing each other. The one time I had tried to needle Bhon, I ended up with a handcannon about two fingers away from my nose. "Surely there were other more well-equipped merchants here. But that is why you lead us, after all. I would never have found such a contract as we are—" She grunted and shifted suddenly, countering the transport's hard turn. That *had* been the wrong street. "—*rocketing* toward. Fortunate indeed."

I had been trying to push down that niggling doubt within myself since I signed the contract. Why did they pick me? I was deciding what to answer, when the speaking tube crackled again.

"Do you want me to burn this engine out? You're going faster than a tree skater with its feet alight. I can only shovel so fast."

"Sorry Saart," I shouted back into the tube. "Almost there." I didn't slow down, though. The border between the Naiyul and Frente sectors was around one more turn, the warehouse not much farther. The disgraced

Naiyul family might have been corrupt, but it was small compared to the major families of Sureri. They had no desire to start a fight they couldn't win, and I used that to my advantage. If a Naiyul made a stink within the borders of an embassy, there would be repercussions I was betting the disgraced family didn't want to deal with.

"How's our tail?" I interrupted the swearing coming from the speaking tube.

"Mine's about to catch fire from all this—" There was a pause. "Oh, you mean..." There was another pause, and I steered between two tall buildings. The streets were smaller here, barely wide enough for the transport. Lucky there was no one coming the other way.

"She's sitting about four buildings back," came Saart's voice, "making some gesture that—oh, now that ain't called for."

I moved the speed indicator lever back down a few notches, gradually bringing the transport to a stop outside a boxy adobe building, larger than most of the others surrounding it. A pipe hissed in the cabin, letting out a buildup of pressure as the old military transport came to a halt. A vent creaked in the other section, and there was a thump that rocked Kamuli forward as the section behind us settled into its final resting place. She took a moment to set her headwrap back to rights, and adjust her jacket.

We waited a few minutes, but I wasn't expecting Amra for some time yet. They would have to go through negotiations, come to a—hopefully reasonable—price, and then unload the cargo before coming here. Best to move slowly.

The weak Sureri sun was not quite fully overhead, and we scouted out the warehouse, looking for anything out of the ordinary. We kicked up small clouds of dust in the barren yard. There wasn't much plant life in this city, and I wondered what the rest of Sureri looked like. Had the great families given the least inhabitable land to their disgraced cousins, or was their whole planet poor in life compared to other homeworlds?

But the yard was empty, and we couldn't stall any longer. The Naiyul official hadn't followed us into the Frente section, so that was one positive. I jerked my head at the warehouse, looming in the empty yard.

"Time to go. Keep your eyes up and your feet light. I intend to be back on Methiem this evening with enough money to think about retiring."

We slid the warehouse door to one side with a screech of rusty skids. Kamuli grunted as she helped me, and I noticed her knives were loose in their sheaths. I waited while my eyes adjusted to the gloom, feeling Saart's fur bristle on my other side, and shivered. This was not the sort of contract I usually took on.

The warehouse was largely empty, skeletons of shelves towering to left and right. The center of the floor was open, but littered with blocky objects, pushed together.

"Anyone there?" I called out. "I was supposed to meet someone to pick up cargo."

A shadow detached from a far wall of the warehouse. I put a hand, palm out, to the others, telling them to wait.

"Eyah, we are here," a voice said in the Trader's Tongue. It had a lilting accent. "Yer just keep yerself cool there, alien, and we'll get the medicine ready."

"Why have they got medicine in this old dingy warehouse?" Saart whispered. "Don't make sense."

I shushed him. The Sureri supplied lots of medicine to the other homeworlds, though it usually went through more official channels. I didn't want to argue with the paycheck, but I had to check the seller's story.

"Medicine for what?" I hoped this Sureriaj would answer the same way.

There was rustling, and a lantern flared to life, making shadows flicker and illuminating five gangly and fair-skinned Sureriaj. They looked as if they had been waiting in this warehouse for months, not hours.

The one in front attempted to smile. I felt Saart bristle beside me. The Festuour and Sureriaj species were not close.

"There is a great epidemic in yer Methiemum cities goin' on. Yer did not know of it?" he asked. "The grand-dame asked yer to make a special run to Methiem, did she?"

"That's right," I said, trying to follow his lyrical accent. "Told me I needed to deliver this to Kashidur City in twenty hours."

"Seventeen now, it is," the lead Sureri said. "Very sensitive to the time passin'. Got to hand it off quick-like." His eyes narrowed. "The epidemic is growin' fast and yer own people are dying. Don't want any o' this gettin' lost before it gets there." Kamuli snorted. As if we would lose cargo.

I put one hand inside my vest pocket, where I kept the directions the well-dressed Sureriaj had given me. I saw the alien's hand twitch, and I pulled the paper out slowly.

"I've got the directions right here—"

"Lemme glance it with me own blinkers," the Sureri said, stepping forward. I tensed, but handed over the paper the gentleman had given me. The alien looked through it carefully, silently sounding out words. I guessed he was able to speak the Trader's Tongue better than he read it.

I hoped he didn't find anything wrong, especially considering the pistols I saw strapped to their thighs. The Sureriaj were even more enamored of the weapons than the Festuour, and unlike Bhon's handcannons, their pistols could fire more than once before being reloaded. If I could get my hand in that market, I wouldn't need to resort to deals like this to turn a profit. The Sureri snapped up projectile weapons from Methiem like a Kirian on a grub. But the circles those merchants moved in were far above my own.

"Eyah, tis right," the alien said shortly, and thrust the paper back at me, adding his own sheaf. "Yer bill of lading. Now pack these crates up nice-like and be off with yer and yer ilk. And make yer sure that fuzzy don't interfere too much, ey?"

He peeled back to the other four Sureriaj, ignoring Saart's snarl, and gestured to twenty large wooden containers—the objects gathered on the open floor of the warehouse. They were almost haphazardly arranged, as if they had been moved here in a hurry and dumped with little purpose or arrangement.

Kamuli and Saart picked up a crate each, and I tucked the paperwork away. Amra would check it later. I could understand the loading bills, of course, but hardly had the patience for it.

I coughed delicately, and the leader's head whipped toward me. I opened my hands to show I meant no harm, and stepped past the others, hoisting a crate. My advance hadn't been expressly clarified in the meeting this morning, so I would be relying on my negotiating skills.

"I must be able to get off-world quickly to deliver this cargo," I began.

"Aye," the leader growled.

"And thus I must schedule the portal to take me to Methiem. Those aren't easy to come by, last minute." I hoped he would take my hint.

"Unless yer plan to cross vasty unknown interstellar distances in some sort of flyin' steam engine, I would agree with yer. And I'm wagerin' ye'd not make it in time."

So that's how it was going to be. "I had to offload my cargo in a hurry to pick up this shipment for you." I told him. "I won't make much profit and I need funds to get me to the drop off point."

The Sureri scowled, looking even more like a grotesque on top of a building. "Me grand-dame did nae specify what to pay yer now," he grumped.

"No, she left that up to me," I told him. "This medicine is important. You said yourself people were dying." This particular member of their species seemed unlikely to be on an errand of mercy. Despite the claim this morning there were no illegal drugs, I wondered if those well-off Sureriaj could be scamming the desperate Methiemum governments about medicine for the epidemic. Were the crates actually filled with drugs like Fuzz or StepUp? I wasn't completely against the odd smuggling job, but that wasn't what I signed up for this morning, especially if my people were suffering from this epidemic. Besides, smuggling required extra planning.

The alien wasn't taking my hint, and I put hands on my hips at the lack of answer. "Do you want it transported or not? If you do, I need the money to move it."

The alien turned away from me abruptly and held a quick conversation with the others. They were certainly his family members—probably all cousins, or maybe a brother or two. He spoke low and fast in the Sureriaj language, so I didn't get more than a few words.

When he turned back to me, he was even paler.

"Eyah, we have enough to cover twenty percent now, the rest-like when yer complete the run. I will have ter inform the grand-dame, yer ken."

I only raised my eyebrows at him. If they freely admitted to having that much, then they had more. They would have planned to give me a small advance. Their family would reimburse them. "Half—to at least cover my expenses."

"Thirty percent. No more for yer until proof of delivery." Oh, this was too easy. Never send a thug to negotiate with a merchant.

I tried on my best innocent-but-not-really face. "It's a question of pure logistics. If I don't get enough money to move these crates, I might have to open them up and sell to the highest bidder to cover my costs." I had intended to get at least get forty percent with this jab, but his eyes widened, his hairy ears coming to points.

"Yer may not open the merchandise!" he snapped. "They must remain sealed to keep the medicine fresh. If we find yer have tampered with any-like part of the crates, me family will find yer and yer other aliens."

I stepped back. I could see a couple of the other aliens reaching for their weapons, and I held up my hands. Threats on a medicine run? What was in those crates? I kept my tone level. "Then I had better have enough to cover everything, and more, don't you think?" I put my hands down, surreptitiously wiping sweaty palms on my leather leggings.

The obviously agitated Sureri turned away again for another *sotto voce* conversation. At least they weren't drawing weapons. Yet.

"Yer are a merchant, no? Yer know how to schedule a portal. We canna be responsible for all yer expenses.

Thirty percent is final."

That would barely be enough. The portals were expensive. I signaled Kamuli, and she put down the box she had picked up. "Then I'm afraid we may have to cancel our business." Now the guns did appear, and I kept myself from moving, tense for the sound of a shot. Careful.

"Yer have signed a contract with me grand-dame," the Sureri said in a low voice. "I donna think yer want to be seen as a contract breaker, do yer?" His men fanned out, showing that they had five to our three.

This would be a fine time for Amra to arrive with Bhon to even the odds.

"There's no need for a broken contract," I said. "Give us the fifty percent up front, and all will go well. I'm sure your grand-dame will—"

"Yer donna talk about our grand-dame!" one of the other Sureri called out, and I swallowed. Seems I'd hit a nerve.

"Fine, fine. This is just business. Simple merchants, negotiating as friends." My hands were at my sides, where I kept a few knives hidden. Kamuli and Saart had stopped all pretense of moving the crates out, and stood on either side of me.

"We will give yer forty percent," the lead Sureri said suddenly. He was watching his brethren, evidently seeing where this negotiation was going. I don't think anyone wanted to try explaining bodies to the Naiyul constables.

And I would have taken that amount, too, a few minutes ago. Now, I was starting to get annoyed.

"I think we'll take the full fifty percent," I said, locking eyes with him.

"Why you—" He switched into his native tongue, and his face went almost white with fury. As he began to reach for his holster, there was a clang behind us, and the Sureri started back.

"Need any help, folks?" came Bhon's voice, and I sagged. She appeared in a stream of light from the open doorway, Amra behind her with a long iron pipe. Bhon had a handcannon in each of her furry paws, and the two flanked us. Five against five.

"Thank you Bhon," I said loudly, "but the nice man here was about to give us fifty percent of our fee up front to keep our delivery timely and *safe*." I watched him, challenging him to another move. He turned to his familymates with a snarl, and the group began handing small bags between themselves.

"Fifty percent," he spat at me, and produced a large bag. By the light chiming sound coming from it, it held the clear unbreakable chips used for trading between the worlds. Nether glass. "If me or me familymates find out yer tampered with the cargo, we will—"

"And who should I go to for the remainder of my fee, once I deliver everything?" I didn't want to know what threat he was going to make. The Sureri sputtered until he got his words going the right direction.

"Yer need to see...to see..." He paused, clearly collecting his thoughts. Sureriaj were touchy about giving out their names, or names of those in their families.

"Ask for...Frente Yatulnath," the Sureri finally managed to say.

I nodded, but by now, I was fairly sure this wasn't the Frente family. We were in the Frente section of the Naiyul trading town, in a run-down warehouse, with five thugs who obviously didn't know much more than we did. I knew the Frente family was fairly liberal in off-world trading—one reason I was willing to take the deal in the first place. These aliens seemed like they would rather trade with sewer rats. Whatever was happening, I doubted the Frente family would appreciate these five Sureriaj, whoever they were, being on their property. My thoughts flashed back to the Naiyul officer following us.

"I will find Yatulnath," I promised, fixing a cheery smile on my face. "I guess I should thank you for this deal, Frente...?" I left the name open for him to complete—an insult, though an uninformed 'alien' wouldn't know that—and watched carefully enough to see him stiffen at the word.

"Eyah, Frente...Masnaith, I am," the Sureri said, not entirely smoothly. He was as Frente as I was. He recovered, sneering. "Yer have seventeen more hours 'til delivery on Methiem. Be on yer way, then, all of yer, and donna let yer dogs mess the floor on the way out."

Kamuli had a hand on Bhon's arm, and from the number of her teeth showing, the Festuour heard the Sureri's last insult. I eyed the false Frente one more time, and guided Saart to the last few crates in the warehouse, making sure he didn't try to start an inter-species war on the way.

Once we were all out, I pulled the warehouse door closed with a screech. Let the false Frentes stew in the dark. I saw the rising questions among my crew and cut them off.

"All the crates into the transport now. We can talk when we have steel walls around us."

There was grumbling, especially from Saart and Bhon, as I helped them pull the last crates into the cargo section. It was full from floor to ceiling, only a small square left to stand in and a narrow corridor down the length. We would have had no room for the spices, and I wouldn't have gotten more than a pittance selling them on my homeworld anyway. I prayed Amra negotiated for a decent amount.

Saart banged the connecting pin to the two halves of the transport with extra vehemence, and Kamuli took the chocks out from the wheels.

When everyone was in—Saart in the engine compartment, Bhon and Kamuli in the living quarters—I closed the heavy steel door of the cockpit shut behind me and threw myself into the co-pilot seat. Amra already had her hands on the control levers, her wrap settled around her.

"Let's go."

We had barely left the warehouse compound when the speaking tube beside the pilot's chair crackled.

"You want to...huff...tell us...huff...why that felt as legal as a...huff...padam made of wood?" Saart was busily shoveling coal as he complained.

There was a wheeze from a second tube, placed above our heads.

"A dog, eh? If the next batch of gargoyles are as pleasant as these they'll be getting my hairy fist in their—" The voice was cut off by Kamuli hushing her mate.

"They do have a point," Amra said.

"Don't you start. Anyway, how did it go with the spices?" I searched the road ahead, but the Naiyul thug who had followed us had fortunately left his post. "Tell me you got something decent for them."

Amra gazed out the windscreen. "How do you do it?" she said, avoiding the question. "Stay so calm in negotiations? I get all flustered the moment someone tells me I'm wrong. I start to doubt myself. I don't suppose I could negotiate while I had my ledger open?" She looked at me with regret and apology on her face.

I sighed, but then wondered how my own negotiations might have gone without Kamuli's imposing presence. No it was better for Amra to have sold the spices, even if we did take a loss.

"I think having your nose in your ledger would take away a bit from your selling presence," I said. She turned the transport carefully around a corner, and tugged her red wrap closer with one hand. "I could never make the numbers dance to my tune like you do."

"And what was the price?" Better to hear the bad news all at once.

"Twenty drezels per ounce."

I tried not to wince, while the Festuour's argument died out over the speakers. "You did good. Next time pretend you're writing all those numbers down in your book rather than staring at the ugly mug you're selling to."

"Next time?" Amra's face lit up and I realized my mistake. I tried to backpedal.

"Yes, well, we have to save up for that little shop on Methiem somehow, don't we? And you have to keep up your habit of supporting whatever orphans and beggar children come our way. Just think, one day, you may even turn a profit! We might have enough to feed a child of our own!"

Amra poked me from the pilot's seat. "I'd give up trying to sell things and be content to write in my little book if you'd agree to marry me *before* we die of old age. We don't have to be stationary to live together. We've done well this far."

I must have looked pained again, because she rolled her eyes. But neither of us got to say anything further.

"There is another Sureri following us." Kamuli's tinny voice cut into our conversation. "He looks like an officer in one of the gangs."

I peered out the window to see the Naiyul official on one of the tall bird-things they favored. Not gaining on us, but just...watching.

Amra frowned. "We had one of the Naiyul constable thugs following us all the way from the market, even though we were doing completely legitimate business. I have all our merchant licenses in order. The protest has everyone acting nervous." She paused, biting her lower lip. "Though Bhon might have taken a little bit of a pot shot at him to keep him from getting too close." That explained the tail.

"Is there something you are not telling us, boss?" Kamuli asked. "What happened when you signed the contract?"

I described the well-to-do grand-dame and her gentleman family member, and how they had presented the contract. It was starting to sound too good to be true. Amra had been right not to trust them. "In any case, those Sureriaj were definitely not Frente." I finished.

"Then what's their game?" Bhon asked through the speaker.

"I don't know," I answered, "but let's get to the portal ground before anything else happens. With the advance they gave us, we can jump the line and get to Methiem today instead of tomorrow. We won't be able to deliver this in time otherwise." And the sooner we got off Sureri, the better.

I held on to my co-pilot's chair as the transport went over a rut in the dirt road with a clang. I heard a grunt from one of the speaking tubes, but other than that my crew was silent, likely contemplating the same questions I was.

The portal ground was on the edge of the trading city, and we lost our shadow by the time we got there. I gripped my chair's arms as Amra brought the heavy transport to a tenuous stop in the line queued at the roped-off square. The transport was good for hauling cargo, not so much for driving through a populated city.

The side hatch clanged open and Saart pulled himself up. "Do I have to say I don't like this?" he asked. He adjusted his glasses. I could hear the engine winding down in the section behind us.

"You just did. And I don't like it either, but it will make us a lot of money." I swiveled my chair, taking in Saart's soot-stained fur. "Or maybe you want to drive this transport back to the warehouse and tell those thugs we've thought better of their deal?"

"No, I want us all to understand what's going on, instead of jumping into a bad deal like a bear into a tar pit. You could have turned this down when you saw the payoff was too large. But you didn't see fit to consult the rest of us."

"I already apologized." I relaxed my grip on the chair, and fought to keep my voice level. "I had to take the contract then or not at all. The profit will cut down the number of new trades before we can look at a shop on Methiem."

Saart snorted. "You'll never settle down."

"Why do you think I took this contract?" I asked.

Amra was pulling levers, letting the transport roll forward in line. "It's a start for him, Saart."

Saart snorted again. "Remember when Prot was 'sick' with the 'Kirian maggot flu?'"

"Yes, when we were supposed to look at potential shopfronts outside Biharia..." Amra turned with a hiss of inhaled air. "Tell me you didn't lie to me."

"So I got cold feet." I raised a hand. "The brakes!" I said, trying to keep the panic out of my voice. There was a cart in front of us with two terrified-looking Lobath.

They were gathering bunches of smushfruit in their arms to cart out of the way.

Amra jerked on the lever, and I barely got my hands up to stop myself flying out of the seat. Saart stumbled into the back of my chair, and I heard a series of grunts and bangs from the passenger section speaking tube.

"That took time and money to set up. If you're so interested in settling down, don't waste my time." Amra was fuming.

"What the hell is going on up—" Bhon began before I flipped the switch next to the speaking tube, cutting her off.

"I'll handle the customs officials," I said, extricating myself from the seat and ignoring both Saart and my accountant. "Get this thing ready to travel to Methiem." I left the cockpit before anyone could catch me and ask any more questions, banging the hatch shut on an enraged squawk from Amra.

I shook my head as I walked. We had to get the merchandise delivered. We had to get the money. We had nothing saved up without it. I pushed away the feeling of impending doom settling on my shoulders.

A few steps away from the transport, I checked the layout of the portal ground. There were four large merchant parties, each with several wooden cargo wagons pulled by system beasts. One set—in the form of immense horses sparkling like glass in the cold sun—doubtless cost more than my transport and cargo combined. The maji-created animals ate grass to sustain themselves, but the cost to recharge the system that ran them was more than I made in a full cycle.

Another group consisted of a pair of Etanela, towering above everyone else, and carrying heavy packs on their backs. Four Kirian women, with short, wildly colored robes ending above wrinkled elbows and knees, talked off to the side. I could see their crests fanning and flattening as they gossiped. There was even one lone Benish, standing rooted to the spot like a particularly gnarled anthropomorphic tree. It carried an immense bag in one hand. All the parties here had surely booked weeks in advance.

I searched the Sureriaj guards, dressed in a combination of family regalia. I could recognize a few—Frente and Baldek, and even one of the Nara family. What I was really looking for was...there. Technically one of the great families, the Naiyul also had a right to put a customs official at the portal ground.

Sureriaj tolerated corrupt family members less than most would tolerate a corrupt employee. Imagine being dragged in front of your company owners and seven of your great-great-grandmothers—who happened to be the same people—to explain why you had taken the money from the nice man with the shiny transport.

As a race, they were loyal to a fault to their family, but the rare individual Sureri was willing to take a little extra on the side. The disgraced Naiyul had fewer ties to family, making them more susceptible.

I checked to make sure none of the other Sureriaj were paying attention before I slipped over to the customs official dressed in the navy and yellow of the disgraced Naiyul. "I need to go through the next portal to Methiem," I said. I took a quick look at the sun. "In the next hour or so, if one's available."

The customs Sureri hefted my proffered clinking bag of Nether glass—a sizeable fraction of the advance I had been paid— and evidently found it acceptable, as he tucked it away with a conspiratorial grin and bent to fill out paperwork. He checked a sheet with timetables, then checked around to make sure the other agents weren't watching before completing the form he gave me. The writing was all in the interconnected Sureri script, but I assumed it was legitimate. I had offered enough.

"Yer in luck, yer are. The majus is makin' a hole to Loba just now, but the next one for them," he threw out a long finger toward the group of Etanela, "is goin' to Kashidur City." He handed me the paper. "Lucky yer leavin' today. Grounds were closed yesterday, what with that protest by the Baldek." He cocked his head to one side. "I'm hopin' yer had a pleasant stay here, regardless."

"Many thanks." At least this Sureri didn't act like I carried fleas. I'm sure the bag of money helped.

I tried not to think of how much the bribe reduced my assets, but it did let us skip the line. Much of the rest would go to the price of the portal itself. I would be expected to share the cost equally with the group of Etanela, so at least they wouldn't complain at our jumping in line. Still, even what Amra got from selling the spices was a valuable addition to our savings at this point.

Without the portals that moved us from planet to planet, the ten homeworlds would have no trade. Just because the maji were the only ones who could open them was no reason to charge so much. Every majus I had seen was rich as a king with an ego bigger than Methiem.

By the time I got back, the others had prepared the transport to travel. I carefully stayed around the other side from Amra, watching Kamuli and Bhon bolt in the last panel to trim down the outline.

My vehicle had been a war machine, in its past life. Its kind had only been used once, more than twenty-five cycles ago, when the Methiem waged a short war against the Sathssn over their trading rights on Sath Home. Turned out preparing the machines for battle, once they passed through portals linking the homeworlds, took so long the Sathssn defeated the Methiemum easily. But we still got the trading rights in the end. That's war for you.

Saart found the transport right after we met, we bought it for a song-and-a-half at a junk yard from a rather eccentric majus, and Saart fixed it up. Physically, it was long and narrow, with low ground clearance. A majus could only open a portal so large, and the transport could only traverse one after modifications to reduce its overall height. The adjustments made riding claustrophobic while in transport mode, but it was worth it to carry cargo between planets. With its capacity, we could rise above many petty merchants, even if we weren't at the level of the larger, better-funded parties.

I sighed. I couldn't avoid things any longer. I stopped pretending to observe my transport, and came around the front of the pilot section at the same time Amra was pulling open the door to the cabin. We stopped, watching each other.

I broke first.

"I shouldn't have lied. I...I wasn't—"

"No, you shouldn't have." Amra interrupted. "If you don't want to settle down yet, tell me. Don't sneak off."

"I wasn't sneaking. I was trying to get our portal scheduled so we can actually make money." I threw a hand back toward the portal ground.

"Oh, and I'm not capable of making us any?"

I frowned. "I never said—" I wanted to tell her how much the money from the spices helped, but before I could, she broke in.

"You were thinking it," Amra accused.

Suddenly, I was angry. I didn't have time for this. "Look, I want you, I want children, I want our store somewhere. We just have to—"

"We've 'just had to' for nearly six cycles," Amra said. "When do we finally find the time to make it happen?"

"I don't know," I shot back. I took the door from her, climbing in. "Maybe when this delivery is finished. Maybe not."

Amra climbed in after me. "We lose money traveling from homeworld to homeworld."

"Then we need this last job to go right," I told her. And a few others. Amra snorted, and took the co-pilot's seat. "Then we can start looking—"

She held up a hand toward me. "I don't want to hear it now. Drive. I can't stand going through portals." Her segue only meant she didn't have a good answer either. But this argument wasn't finished.

I pushed any retorts to the back of my mind, and checked through the speaking tubes that everyone was strapped in. Driving to the front of the line, I saw the portal to Loba closing, the hole in the air compressing to nothing.

The majus standing in front of our transport—a red-skinned fishy-looking Lobath—went to the group of Etanela, asking a question. A bag of coins changed hands. She shivered in the cold, the wind puckering her rubbery skin. Her three long tentacles growing in place of hair were drawn close to shield her from the wind. Next she came to us, calling in the Trader's Tongue through the side door I had left open.

"You are going to Methiem, yes? You agree to split the cost with the other party?"

"We are, and we do," I called back. Amra counted out the fee in Nether glass we got from the Sureriaj, not looking at me. The amount was much bigger than that of the bribe. I eyed it with distaste, wondering where the money went. A bribe to smooth our transit was one thing, but the cost of traveling from one homeworld to another was far too high, in my estimation.

Amra handed the pouch to the majus, who hefted it with a practiced hand and gestured us forward. I kept the transport idling right behind the group on foot. Amra shut the door and, despite our argument, a thrill ran through me. This never got old.

The Lobath majus walked to the front of the line, but before she could do anything, there was a disturbance behind us, and I looked out the window near my seat. Four of the Naiyul constables pushed through the waiting line, each riding a tall bird.

"These aliens are not allowed to leave our world," the one who had tailed us said. He must have gone back to get reinforcements.

I didn't have time for this. I went to the hatch, rolling it back to argue, but the majus got there first.

"What is the suspicion?" she asked. "You have a warrant for them, yes?"

The Sureri faltered. "They've been hangin' 'round warehouses, and we think they mebbe have stolen goods..."

"We're merchants," I shouted. "We hang around warehouses for a living. Do you have proof or not?" I could see others in line starting to talk and shuffle. The Sureri constable was going to have another riot on his hands if he wasn't careful.

"They have already paid for portal," the Lobath majus said. "I must make it now, unless you have proof."

The Sureri made a horrible face at me. "We know yer involved," he said. "We'll track yer down soon, don't fret."

I traded looks with Amra, our argument swept aside for the moment.

The majus turned her back on the constables and waved vaguely in midair, doing her magic. The black oblong hole between worlds opened, and I climbed back in my seat. Unless the Sureri physically stopped the transport, there was nothing they could do. Anything to get off this world.

They *had* been watching us, but why? The cargo? We just needed to deliver it, get our money, and all would be well.

I drove away from the constables, away from Sureri, and past the majus. The Etanela we shared the portal with were a bit taller than the transport, and ducked to pass through the top edge of the portal. The majus had skimped on the height to make it wide enough for us. I kept the wheels turning slowly, aimed directly for the slice of utter blackness, barely high enough for the curved and aerodynamic outline of the transport. My arms broke into gooseflesh as I tried not to think about the two halves of the transport separated by the distances between homeworlds.

The cabin passed through the hole in the air, and in the briefest flash of black, the chill desert afternoon of Sureri turned to a warm spring morning near Kashidur City on Methiem. I felt something loosen in my chest. It felt good to be home.

Customs

- Official portal grounds are tightly regulated by homeworld customs agents. However, it is impossible to tax all trading on each homeworld, which encourages smuggling. Most illegal goods are local to the world. Pertinent issue for discussion concerns small percentage of goods smuggled through portals between homeworlds. Goods not available or manufacturable on one homeworld will be worth more when sold there. Rare reports exist of maji bribed to pass goods through unofficial portals, though claims are not yet supported. If confirmed, would lead to heavy disciplinary action by the Council of the Maji.

Summary of Great Assembly session topic, third gathering of the second quarter, 997 AAW

I f I had my way, I would have driven out of the portal grounds and been to the city in a few minutes. But Methiem is the biggest trading planet of the ten homeworlds, and Kashidur City the biggest trading port. The customs officials were depressingly good at their job, as I had learned more than once when passing through my home planet with goods of a...delicate...nature.

This shipment particularly bothered me, and the assurances of the well-dressed Sureriaj and his grand-dame who had bought my services were starting to lose their ring of truth. But no matter how strange the circumstances of the transaction, I had to believe the time and effort of whichever family was pretending to be the Frente did not simply consist of a plot to land me in a prison in Kashidur City. I wasn't worth that much. I wiped at my forehead.

"Are you sweating?" Amra asked. We were at a standstill behind a line of travelers, and I had the parking lever crammed upward to keep the transport from rolling forward.

"I'm beginning not to like this delivery." If everything went well, they'd take a look at the cargo compartment, Amra would give them our bill of lading, and we'd be on our way. I prayed the Sureriaj had finished all their documentation.

"Beginning?" Amra asked. I could tell by her tone she was still angry. "I haven't ever liked it—what?" She must have seen me start. With our fight, and the quick ride to the portal ground, I had never given her the sheaf of paper from the false Frentes.

I patted the pockets of my vest swiftly, my shoulders slumping as I found the papers in my left breast pocket where I'd put them. By now Amra was staring at me.

"With everything that happened, I forgot to—"

There was a clang, and Kamuli opened the pilot section hatch to interject her very large, very dark, frame into the cockpit. "Boss, you should come see the cargo." Her rich, precise tones sent a shiver through me. Our time was running down and we didn't need any more upsets.

I thrust the papers at Amra with a growl. "Check these." I stood up and exited the transport with Kamuli.

Kaumli jogged past the engine and living compartments, her knives clacking as she ran, one hand on her headwrap. "Why are we running, and why couldn't you tell me this before I was in line to have my earwax inspected by Methiemum customs?"

"We only just found it." As usual, she betrayed no

anger at my accusation. Kamuli was never a good target for my frustration.

If only I hadn't been in such a hurry to leave Sureri. If only I hadn't fought with Amra. If only I had all the riches of a majus.

I eyed the line for customs. There was a whole mess of Lobath merchants up front, head-tentacles tied in intricate knots, milling around a creature like an octopus mated with a circus tent. I'm not sure how it came through a portal, but the officials would be several minutes before they were through. Live animals were always troublesome to bring to other homeworlds.

There were several other groups behind them: Methiemum with carts filled with goods, a few wealthy Festuour and Lobath families, obviously on a vacation, the Etanela who came from Sureri in front of us, even a small group of Sathssn, dark cloaks showing no hint of their skin, leading a line of lizard-like pack beasts.

Bhon was in the cargo section, standing guard over the wooden crates. Her green-yellow fur was already drooping in the humid air on Methiem, and I knew Saart's would be doing the same, though he was more used to it from operating the transport's engine. Their homeworld was more akin in temperature to the Sureri trading port in many places, though not as dry.

"What do you want to show me?" I asked, tucking my shirt back in after our brief exercise. A trickle of sweat ran down my back.

"It's smack dab in the middle of one of the crate panels," Bhon told me, her bright blue eyes sharp. "But that side was turned down when we loaded it up—I think those gargoyles planned it that way. I only picked up on it 'cause the crate didn't sit right."

The twenty crates were stacked up to the low ceiling, two by two. There was barely enough room for us to stand, Kamuli with one foot outside the hatch. The crate in question was pulled into the small open space of the cargo segment. My transport was spacious for what it was, but Kamuli's head brushed the ceiling, and it was barely wide enough for all three of us to stand side by side.

The crate, about one arm's length wide, had been turned with the offending side up. A flat hexagonal panel was attached to the surface.

"Any idea what it is?" I asked.

"None," Kamuli told me. "It is not a mechanism, nor is it biological in nature. I do remember the crates felt odd when we moved them into the train." Bhon nodded her agreement.

I realized I had tightened my shoulders again, and was grinding my teeth together. So much for the relaxing passage through the portal. I had an inkling of what the hexagon might be, but hoped I was wrong.

"Anything strange with the cargo?" I asked. At Bhon's bark of a laugh, I amended, "Anything *else* strange?"

"There's one more thing we found," she said, taking out her handcannon. I started moving the instant I saw what she intended, but too late. The crack of the shot was a physical thing in such a confined space, and I instinctively ducked to avoid a ricocheting bullet.

"Look, boss." Her voice cut through the ringing in my ears.

I raised my head at Bhon's words to see the projectile still traveling toward its target. The little lump of metal slowed to a crawl, covering the distance by halves and thirds, as if traveling through thick molasses. Several seconds later, the bullet gently touched the side of the crate and fell with a *tink* to the floor. I eyed Bhon, wondering how exactly she knew what the bullet would do.

"The customs crew isn't going to like this," I said, reaching out to hover my palm over the little hexagonal plate. It was giving off just enough heat to feel, as if it had stolen the energy from the bullet.

"Is it of the maji?" Kamuli asked.

"Unfortunately," I said. I realized I was still tensing my jaw and tried to relax.

Those who travel off their home planet know the maji create the portals allowing us to travel the ten homeworlds. The portals, and the maji enable us to have the Great Assembly of Species, which is the absolute authority on anything inter-species in nature.

But that is the least of what the maji can do. They're responsible for creating the system beasts and many other magical constructs. They help out in times of disaster and strife, displaying awesome powers to change the nature of reality.

Each of the ten planets has their own small share of maji. Some are even minor celebrities, like the Etanela racer Mierla Utelu Tadeti, or the Kirian actor Havrasta Kyliner. Fewer people know the maji separated themselves into houses, each concerned with a different concentration of ability.

"You can't open any of the crates." I guessed.

Bhon's eyes widened. "How'd you know that?"

"Lucky guess." I was fairly sure the hexagonal panels were artifacts made by a majus of the House of Potential, but I didn't have time to tell the pair *how* I knew. I tested my theory, attempting to lift the lid of the crate. By the time I touched the wood, my fingers were tingling and I hardly had strength to pull my hand away. I rubbed my numb appendage. "All of them are like this?"

"Even with a crowbar," Kamuli muttered, and Bhon grimaced up at her. Bhon tended to get carried away sometimes.

Masnaith shouldn't have been so concerned about us opening the crates. There must have been a countering effect at the warehouse, allowing the crates to be loaded and moved. He probably hadn't understood what it did.

"Medicine," Bhon grunted.

"I imagine it *is* a particular kind of medicine," Kamuli supplied. "But not for the sickness on Methium. Instead, it is one our buyer does not want us to know about, or take any 'samples' for our own use."

"No, the grand-dame herself insisted this wasn't drugs, and paid us a lot to deliver them quickly." This wasn't sitting right with me. "She might not have been Frente, but I don't think she lied about that part. It can't be that simple." What was in these things? Now I was going to have to break into this cargo.

Unfortunately, that was when the transport began to rumble forward.

Leaving the two bodyguards with the boxes, I exited the cargo section and ran alongside the slowly moving vehicle, pulling myself out of the dust and back into the pilot cabin. Amra was in the pilot seat.

"We're up," she said, smoothing her red wrap. This morning on Sureri seemed like days ago. "You took too long back there, so I took the pilot's chair to not rouse any extra interest." Her voice was businesslike. She still hadn't forgiven me, not that I could blame her.

"Thanks," I said, without much enthusiasm. The Lobath and their octopus circus tent were gone, as were a few groups behind them. A selection of Festuour leading a string of fuzzy bovines were finishing up.

"Amra," I started, "I'm sorry I lied. I really do want

to settle down with you. It's just—"

"It's always 'just,'" she answered, then shook her head, still concentrating on driving the transport. "Not now. We don't have time to argue about it, and we're *going* to come to an agreement this time, one way or the other." She flashed a look at me and I sat back. With that face, I could wait.

The line must have been longer than usual, as the customs officers were splitting up, checking on each group to make sure their transition would be smoother than the Lobath's. There's always that one unprepared group. I had a feeling we would be another.

Our transport caught the attention of an old and hostile looking woman in the green and brown of the Methiemum homeworld customs. Her light gray hair was pinned in a bun, and her mouth looked permanently stuck in a frown.

I kept my footing while Amra slowed the transport. She thrust the bill of lading back at me. "Everything looks official," she said. "I'm glad *one* of us took the time to read it. I assume there was nothing wrong with the cargo? Did Kamuli give a false alarm?"

I snorted a bitter laugh and took the documentation from her. "I'm sure we won't be thrown in prison at all."

"What's that supposed to mean?"

I ignored Amra, hopping down from the pilot's section and handing the bill of lading to the customs woman, who investigated it for several moments. She was waiting far enough outside the door to give me space to get down, but no farther. Keep the suspect from running.

"What are you carrying today—" she glanced down, "—Prot?"

"Cargo for delivery," I told her with as much confidence as I could muster. "Medicine from Sureri for the ongoing epidemic of the Shudders." The grand-dame and her family would have alerted the medical centers this shipment was coming. "I'm planning to take it to the storage facility as soon as I get out of customs."

The woman's frown deepened, her bottom lip in danger of climbing into her mouth. "We've already received the scheduled delivery of anti-seizing capsules. It was early today." She pulled a clipboard from under her arm. "And the inflammation reducing poultices are being delivered in two days' time."

My heart sank with every word. "It's an extra shipment? It was a rush job, very urgent." I tried to exude official-ness. Surely the grand-dame sent word ahead. The one who signed a false family name to the document. The one who wanted me to move the cargo as soon as possible, as in *before* the official delivery. I carefully kept my face neutral. I really hoped it wasn't drugs.

Her expression didn't change. "Either way I'll have to inspect the items. We'll figure out what those Sureri are sending, won't we, Prot?"

I winced. What could I do? I usually dealt with art, or foodstuffs, or furniture, not with sensitive and potentially harmful items. I gestured helplessly to my cargo section and the old woman limped toward it.

Kamuli or Bhon—probably Kamuli—had enough sense to turn the crate artifact side down. They had their best innocent faces on and I jerked my head for them to wait outside. The cargo section would be crowded enough without them.

The woman began her inspection, counting and touching the crates, but soon grunted in frustration. "I can't get any of these crates open, Prot. How are they secured?"

"I'm just transporting this, as I told you," I said. "My

supplier was fairly adamant I not open the crates. I guess they locked them up well. Perishable maybe." I looked out the hatch, keeping my face neutral. "I hadn't checked."

The woman eyed me. Her hair was stark white at her temples, and her tanned skin as wrinkled as a Kirian. It was a marvel she was still working. But her eyes were keen as a well-sharpened blade.

"Were they," she drawled. "Hadn't you." She strode past me in the confined cargo compartment. "We'll get the majus to investigate this," she grated over her shoulder as she exited. "Move your vehicle to the side, and we'll pass you through as soon as she determines there is nothing of the maji tied to this cargo."

I held out a hand to the woman's retreating back, but let it fall as she disappeared outside the hatch. She moved fast for an old lady.

The willowy Methiemum woman serving at the portal grounds soon arrived. She took one look at the crates—or at something around them—and turned back to the customs woman, puffing up the ladder behind her. Kamuli and Bhon were still outside, undoubtedly listening, and I remained where I was, emitting beams of pure innocence.

"This is work of the House of Potential," the majus said smoothly in a fluid accent. She must have been from somewhere on the northern continent, possibly even from Ibra. I suspected most of what this majus said or did was smooth. Her actions were graceful, almost as if she was swimming. Her clothes were expensive, finely tailored and ornamented with silver inlay. About what I would expect from one of the elite magic-users.

"Which means what?" the customs woman asked.

"It is a complex arrangement of the Symphony, but that is all I can tell you." The majus pulled her long hair back over her shoulders.

"Whoever put you up to transporting this was concerned about keeping it secret, Prot," the official told me. I was getting annoyed at her continual use of my name. They were probably trained to do it to convey friendship. It wasn't working. "Anything with this level of security on it needs to be investigated."

"Can you open them?" I asked the majus. I could hedge to the recipients later, assuming I wasn't arrested. I just had to get these crates delivered in time and get my money. And never take a contract from a Sureri again.

"Of course not." She flicked a hand in my direction as if shooing a fly. "I am of the House of Grace."

"We'll have to impound your vehicle while we call for a majus from the House of—" The customs woman looked to the majus.

"House of Potential," the finely dressed majus said.

"Potential," the old woman repeated. "Right."

"My replacement is arriving in a few hours, but he is of the House of Strength, and will not be able to help," volunteered the majus uselessly.

"I have to deliver this cargo by tomorrow morning," I told them. "If you want someone to inspect it, it'll have to be now."

"Your supplier should have thought of that before they set this up," the customs woman countered. "Unless you can find a majus of the House of Potential, your delivery will be coming in late."

I stared back at them, remembering when Saart and I first bought the old war machine. Who we bought it from. I must have stood longer than I thought.

"Prot?" The customs woman looked vaguely worried.

I swallowed. "I may know of one, but he's retired." I hoped he still lived in the same place. I hoped he was still alive. I hadn't seen the man in multiple cycles.

"I don't know of any maji living near here," the majus sniffed.

"You don't know everything, missy." The old customs woman mumbled something sounding like 'stuck up maji.'

The majus harrumphed and flounced out of the train and I smirked at the customs woman despite myself. There was more to this old bag than I thought.

"Will you let me fetch him?"

The old lady considered, but our mutual dislike of the pampered majus must have improved her perception of me. "Move your vehicle out of the way. Only you may leave." It was a start. We exited the cramped compartment and I closed the hatch behind us.

"May I unhook the pilot and engine section to get there faster? My mechanic has to keep the engine running." If she didn't let me, there was no way I could get there in time. I might as well wait for the official majus.

The woman's face scrunched up until I thought her mouth would disappear entirely, but she scanned the line of travelers passing through customs. Kashidur City had more visitors than any other city on Methiem, and it was a busy day. While we had been in the cargo section, five more groups had come through portals—one was a gaggle of Kirian schoolchildren, their robes a whirlwind of conflicting colors, crests fluttering and changing as they pointed excitedly around them. Their teacher, an older woman with the trademark wrinkled and liverspotted Kirian skin showing on her bare arms and legs, was trying to herd them. Her feathery crest looked as if was trying to go in all directions at once.

"I'll have to process more paperwork." The woman sounded as if she would rather cut off her own leg, but we both knew it would get me out of her hair sooner. "Wait here."

While she waded through the red tape of the Methiem customs bureaucracy, I filled my crew in on what had happened.

"And you know of a majus in the city other maji do not?" Kamuli asked. I had been hoping that question wouldn't come up.

"It's a long story," I said, and Saart nodded beside me, his eyebrows raised. "Suffice to say we bought the transport from him, a long time ago."

"Another story you haven't shared?" Amra suggested.

I sighed, but she was right. "I'll tell you when I get back, when we have that talk. Promise."

"Whenever you two want to stop bickering and get back to making us money is fine with me," Bhon said, furry arms crossed. I looked around my crew, seeing agreement from the other two. I took Amra's hand. She didn't pull away, at least.

"I will make this up to you, I promise," I told her. She didn't seem mollified.

By the time the woman came back with her paperwork, we had unhitched the front two sections and Saart was priming the engine. I signed the necessary documents, in triplicate, saying my cargo was forfeit if he and I decided to make a run for it. The thought only crossed my mind for an instant.

"Amra is in charge while I'm gone." I hesitated for an instant. "Unless some transaction comes up, then Kamuli is." I still wanted to make money, after all.

My accountant's eyes were alight when I climbed

into the pilot's seat. "This had better be worth the money," she whispered as I went past her. Her voice had an edge.

"Enough to start us toward a storefront," I told her. Maybe with just one or two more deliveries. "Think of our little shop, a couple kids underfoot. I'll be back before you know it." She glared back, but at least didn't slam the hatch.

Saart and I rumbled out of a side door in the wooden fence surrounding the customs area, and turned to the city. Its skyline rose above me, the largest mercantile firms in the city center over twenty stories tall. Another huge building was in the midst of construction, scaffolding covering the metal exterior. Where the structure showed through, the polished steel gleamed in the morning sunlight. No other city I knew of had so much metal in once place.

"Did you have to tell Amra about the Kirian maggot flu?" I asked him.

The speaking tube between the pilot and engine sections crackled a moment before Saart's voice came through, gruff as usual.

"Boy, you've been tiptoeing around that girl for the last six cycles. Would you have ever told her if I didn't?"

I thought about that a moment. "Probably not."

"Then it's a good thing I did. I may not have a lady-friend myself, but I know how to treat one. If she leaves, our books are going to be as muddled up as they were when you were in charge of them, and no one wants that." Not to mention what it would do to me.

I blew out a breath. Saart stayed out of the money—and relationship—side of the business as much as possible. But when he decided to comment, the old Festuour was usually right.

"Fair comment," I said. And we left it at that.

The two of us consulted over the speaking tube as I drove and he shoveled coal. We bought the transport almost fourteen cycles ago, just after we met. I had been a fresh-faced teen, Saart older, but fed up with working in a repair shop on Festuour. We met in a bar one night, hit it off, decided to go into business, and never looked back.

Between the two of us, we figured out where the old junkyard had been, on the outskirts of Kashidur City. If it was still there.

It took the better part of two hours to find it, tucked away between a warehouse storing bins of minerals and ore, and a newly constructed store selling replacement parts for wagons and transports. The yard was smaller than I remembered. I could see the ridge of another vehicle like ours, but this one rusted beyond use, with a hole blown in one side large enough to run through. The transport we bought had been in better shape than most.

We pulled into the yard to a chorus of dogs barking. The junkyard mutts were all chained up, though well taken care of. I hopped down from the pilot's cabin. A few moments later Saart huffed down the stairs from the steam engine, wiping coal dust from his glasses off on his fur.

"Well, now what?" He adjusted his bandolier and glasses, though I saw he had unbuttoned a couple pockets to make sure his larger, heftier tools were within reach. He didn't have the same attraction to guns Bhon did.

"Now we hope the old coot is still alive," I answered.

We threaded a path through the junk. Someone was obviously here. The dogs would have been loose to guard the yard if they were out. Saart pointed to a little shack, hidden behind a stack of broken cartwheels. I had vague memories of finishing our business deal to buy the transport in there. The piles of broken parts and garbage had grown since then, almost covering the building. As we progressed, the path narrowed, until we were slithering sideways between stacks. I heard Saart grunt as he pushed through two piles of broken tile shingles, stacked on top of each other.

The entrance to the building was blocked by the huge, outreaching forelimb of a system beast carcass, evidently too run-down to be useful. The junkyard owner must have been working on it. This one was shaped like one of the predatory thrycovolars of equatorial Festuour, long drained of any magical energy and fallen on its side. I reached out to move the jointed forepaw to clear the doorway, but my hand went dead as I touched the beast. I pulled it back sharply, shaking it, holding it to my chest.

"What? What happened?" Saart was next to me in an instant, looking me over.

"We've reached the majus," I told him. The feeling was starting to come back to my hand. There was no way we could get to the building without moving the beast, or at least its forearm. "Help me shift this thing."

"Hey in there!" called Saart. "Do you want customers or not?"

No answer.

"Come on. Even if he doesn't, we have to see him." I put my shoulder to the bear-cat monster's foreleg. The feeling in my arm started to drain away, but the layers of clothing in between helped. Saart didn't have that luxury, and hissed through his pointed teeth as he pushed. Time was wasting, but by resting every few moments, the feeling would come back to our extremities, and the forepaw, as big around as my body, began to move with a shrill squeak. Once it was out of the way, there would be enough room to slip through.

"Almost there!" Saart said, and gave a final heave with his considerable bulk. With a screech, the paw jerked forward and I, one hand outstretched, fell face-first into the body of the thrycovolar.

I felt suddenly weak and sleepy, and blackness descended. Strange dreams invaded, of cold lands and metallic horrors, with a treasure guarded by magic and bat-faced shadows dressed in rags.

"Wake up." I swam toward the gravelly voice, and opened my eyes. I was confronted with a shaggy, none too clean face, surrounded by long unkempt hair—it was older, but familiar. As my head cleared, I saw we were inside the little shack. Had Saart carried me in?

"My little surprise traps most who try to find me," the bewhiskered man said. He was wearing a shaggy brown leather cloak, buttoned down the front, and not much else. Bare, dirt-encrusted feet poked out from beneath it. Even inside the shack, there were piles of junk. "But Prot, if you wanted to visit, you should have sent word ahead."

I thrust away the last of the dreams. Did the old majus actually remember my name from our one business deal fourteen cycles ago? I looked to Saart, sitting gingerly on a pile of broken tables. He shrugged. The man had been strange when we first met him.

"How is the war transport treating you?" The man was looking me over as if I was a long-lost son, not a customer. "Still running smooth? I see you lost a couple sections since the last time we met."

"I...no, we haven't lost..." I paused, gathering my thoughts. I pressed one hand to my left eye. The field on the broken system beast had been like those on the crates, sucking away energy. That convinced me we were in the right place, though I wished I hadn't fallen into it. "That's why we're here. We need your help."

The man looked confused for a moment. "With the transport? I have some spare parts, but..." He gestured with one gnarled hand at the junkyard in general.

"With what's in the other two sections," Saart said. His nose was wriggling as if he smelled something off. "We need a majus."

The man snorted. "I don't do that anymore. Gave up the whole pomp of it for peace and quiet out here." His words were punctuated by his dogs, barking at the transport.

"But—" I pointed a thumb back to the door.

"Yes, there are exceptions," he snapped, and just for a moment, I saw the regal bearing of a majus, before the man slumped again. "I don't have much of my song left. Spent too much when I was young and now I'm reduced to tinkering in my junk piles here."

"We only need your help for a few hours—" I fumbled for a name.

"Call me Colonel," he said. I remembered he had gone by his rank before. He had been in the Methiemum army, back in the war with the Sathssn. Probably how he came across so many of the ill-fated transports.

"Colonel," I agreed. "We need you to open some cargo crates for us. They've been sealed by another majus of the House of Potential. There are none who can be spared and the cargo is time sensitive. Saart and I wondered if you could help." It was how we knew so much about the House of Potential. The Colonel had still acted as majus then.

"Time sensitive, eh?" The Colonel scratched at his dirty beard with one hand, dislodging a small shower of dandruff. "As in expensive?"

I sighed, wondering how much this would cost me. "They're medical supplies ordered for the victims of the Shudders epidemic ravaging the southern continent," I told him, without much hope of it helping.

"So you're saying you'll be paid well by a government institution for delivering emergency supplies on time," he said. "We can discuss my price when we get there."

Saart threw up his hands and stalked out of the shack, grumbling. I signaled for the old majus to follow.

The trip back was uneventful, and much shorter, now I knew where I was going. Fortunate as well, as the Colonel had a rather unique odor. He gabbed on the whole time, remarking how well the transport was kept up, asking Saart keen questions about the engine, and occasionally poking at one of the buttons on the dash. I didn't even know there were shutters to close the front windows. It would have been more helpful if I had not found out while driving.

The same old woman let us back into the customs area, and I backed the cab and engine in front of the other two sections. As we emerged, the woman eyed the majus with her usual frown and one raised eyebrow. He was dirty, ragged, and hairy. Not in any way the upright symbol the maji liked to present to the universe. He nodded back, as if this was all familiar to him. It might have been—he could have been stationed here, long ago, to open portals. They might have even met each other.

"Let's get this...majus to open those crates, Prot," she said, pushing us toward the cargo section. "You're blocking up my area." She was at least willing to let the Colonel through, but I could practically feel her disbelief.

The others crowded around as we walked. "Is that

the majus you bought the transport from?" Amra asked, tucking her wrap in close so no one would step on it.

"Pretty sure," I said. "Otherwise I'm going to have a dirty beggar I found in a junkyard inspecting my cargo. That and he knocked me unconscious with a magical trap."

"Are you—?" she started, and I waved the question away.

"Just...strange dreams." The images while I was unconscious unsettled me. This job was playing with my head. I looked to the sun, but it was far past where I had hoped. We arrived on Methiem in the morning, but had spent much of the day at a standstill. Of our original twenty hours, there was maybe half that time left. Could we deliver the cargo at night? Would we want to? I wasn't sure I wanted to be in a dark warehouse with whoever was supposed to receive this cargo.

The offending crate was still in the middle of the cargo section. Bhon and Kamuli had heavy wool gloves to protect their hands, one pair for three-fingered Festuour and one for Methiemum, and turned the crate so the plate was visible on top again. The customs woman grunted at this, but said nothing, as the Colonel creaked up the stairs to the rear hatch.

He bent over the box, fingers hovering a mere hairsbreadth away from the strange plate. I glanced down at my own hand, remembering the tingling when I touched the device and the system beast. The majus seemed to suffer no such setbacks, although his face fell.

He looked at me, and it was as if all the raggedness and dirt fell away. "I can open this," he said, "but I have a price."

Always maji, and their prices.

"What?" I said through gritted teeth. Our remaining funds were running low. The more I spent, the more

Amra and I quarreled. Our little store was drawing away like a stone sinking to the bottom of a deep pool.

"You must do the right thing with this cargo, Prot," the Colonel told me. "It is imperative you succeed. Much more rests on your decision than you think."

We all stared at him, but his face was deadly serious. My heart lifted a little at the lack of monetary compensation, but there was such earnestness in his face. Well, hadn't I always done the right thing, minus a few smuggling runs? I would admit to occasionally taking advantage of a gullible customer, but somehow I knew the majus was not talking about that. I met his eyes.

"I promise," I said, and my crew looked at me as if I was speaking nonsense.

With a click, the little shape on top of the crate cracked in two, and we all jumped save the Colonel. He picked up both pieces and reverentially gave them to Bhon.

"Let's see what's inside of these here crates," he said.

With evening fast approaching, Bhon levered the top off the crate, the only resistance to her crowbar that of the nails.

We all looked in on the nest of shavings and little glass jars.

"Medicine," Bhon said.

Kamuli helped her pull the top away. "She is right, as far as I can tell." She dug one dark hand into the crate, shifting wood shavings aside, bringing out a jar filled with small pills.

The customs woman leaned forward through the hatch, clipboard and pen held ready. "Those are the anti-seizing drugs, though I don't know why there's an extra delivery," she said. "And the others?"

"We can't open all of them," I told her. "I'm liable to

lose payment already for this one."

"I have to make sure," she said stubbornly. "This one could be a decoy."

I cast about, my gaze landing on the Colonel. "Could you open all of them?" It would take time we didn't have, but if the first crate passed inspection, the others should as well.

"No." The Colonel shook his head. "I don't have that much song left." I closed my eyes.

"But I can do one better." He pushed through Kamuli and Bhon, raising one old hand to trail along the boxes. He shuffled along the narrow path to the rear of the cargo compartment, turned, and came back the other direction, his other hand now making a rasp as it slid down the wooden surfaces. As he got closer, I saw his eyes were closed and his head was cocked slightly, as if he was listening to a faraway song.

"By their energy potential, the crates all contain the same thing," he pronounced. "Each is filled with containers, and each container has a supply of dense manufactured pellets." He took one more step forward and took the glass jar from Kamuli, considering. He closed his eyes again, his right ear next to the jar. Then he put his head to the nearest crate.

"Yes. As far as I can tell, they all contain the same objects as this one." He opened his eyes again. "Will that satisfy you? This delivery is as urgent as he says."

The old customs woman drew in her eyebrows, but agreed. "It'll have to do. It seems you are clear, Prot. I hope you are still in time." She gave the old majus a stern glare, ripped off a signed piece of paper from her clipboard, gave it to me, and exited the transport. I followed her, but the Colonel cleared his throat loudly.

I stopped, and exhaled, gesturing my guards out. "Take that jar with you," I told Kamuli. The majus nodded at my action.

"You want me to do something else with this medicine," I told him when we were alone, "and that's going to cut into my profits even more. What do you know?"

But the majus only smiled sadly. "I told you I'm out of that business. I no longer get involved in these things, Prot. Bad for my health." He scratched at his beard. "Speaking of which, my pension from the Council of the Maji has long since run out. Surely twelve percent isn't too much to spare for keeping you on time."

"Barely on time," I countered. "I can spare five percent, and that's it. More than that and my accountant will injure me greatly." How many more jobs would we need before we could stop traveling the homeworlds? After this delivery, staying on Methiem was starting to sound better all the time.

"Make it ten and we have a deal," the Colonel said.

"Seven, and I try to 'do the right thing' with this cargo." I stared at him a moment, trying to divine by sheer will what the old man had meant by that. For all I knew he wanted me to give the medicine away, but I didn't think so, based on his willingness to take my money. He stared back impassively for a moment, then spread one hand in agreement.

I turned away. "I'll get your payment," I told him, and went down the stairs.

Behind me, I heard him call to Amra. "Come help an old man down out of this thing." She went to him, and stood talking while I got my last pouch of Nether glass. He might tell her the story of how we bought the transport. He liked to talk enough.

When I returned, Amra gave me a funny look and

went to the pilot's section. I gave the Colonel the pouch and he hefted it with one hand, a little grin on his dirty face. "What was all that about?" I asked.

He shook his head. "Simply imparting some advice to your lovely accountant. Good luck. And be careful. I can find my own way back."

I wasn't planning on taking him back to his junkyard. I turned away with a halfhearted wave, calling to get the transport ready to roll out of the customs yard. We had taken far too long, I didn't want to make the delivery at night, and now I had a mystery to follow up on.

While the others connected the sections of the transport, I investigated the jars myself. Each glass container was marked discretely on the side with the crest of the Sureriaj family that had made it: Nara, Frente, Baldek, Perchet. I sifted through the crate, taking one from each house, but counting up fractions in my head.

Three of the great families who had contributed to this shipment were fairly liberal with regard to aliens. The Baldek were not. What were they doing sending medicine offworld? I wondered what 'Frente' Masnaith's true name had been.

I took a few more of the Baldek-marked jars, just to make sure, one each from the other houses, set them aside, and closed up the crate. I heard the *thunk* of the connecting bolt between sections and took the jars with me.

"All ready?" I asked Saart outside.

He tucked a hefty wrench away in his bandolier and nodded, adjusting his glasses with his other hand. "We going to get these things delivered tonight? Don't have many hours left."

"No." By the lack of reaction, he wasn't surprised. His glance trailed over the jars I had tucked in my arms. "But the warehouse is on the other side of Kashidur city.

Let's park on the outskirts tonight so we can be ready to deliver these Vish-cursed things at first light. We'll still be within our time limit." Barely.

Saart's bright blue eyes watched me behind his glasses. "Anything you say." He went to start the steam engine.

I secreted my collection of glass jars in a blanket in my bunk so they wouldn't rattle, and went to the pilot section. I let the others know we would be stopping for the night and making the delivery in the morning.

Saart kept the engine going, and Bhon and Kamuli rode in their usual place in the living section. Amra, of course, was beside me in the co-pilot's chair. We rode in silence as the sun dipped below the horizon, and the gaslights started to flicker on in Kashidur City, lighting our way. We had our own lamps on top of each section. Two more on the transport's nose spilled illumination before us.

Halfway around the city, Amra spoke.

"I've been noting down our expenses." There wasn't an overt question attached, but I knew what she meant.

"I gave the last of our upfront bonus to the majus," I told her. "Seven percent. You should add that to the total." I was contemplating numbers in my head, and I didn't like where it was going. I could be wrong.

Amra calculated for a few moments, peering at her ledger in the dim light reflected from the front lanterns. "Don't tell me the number," I said. "We don't have enough to even think about buying a shop."

"We wouldn't have enough even without these expenses. You keep going on about our shop. You know I'm happy to travel in the transport for now. Did you ever mean to buy a place?"

Saart's warning flashed through my mind. He was right. It was time to change things.

"No." I glanced over to see her mouth set, eyes fixed on her accounts. "Not at first. But I do now, Amra, I really do." She raised her face, but still didn't look at me.

I thought about my discovery with the jars. "I'm done with the traveling game," I told her. "After the last four months on Loba, and the week on Sureriaj, I'm done trying to scrabble for a living, taking what we can from the maji, and the homeworld governments, and their customs bureaucracy. Make the customers come to us, if they want what we have. We'll have a little garden out back of the shop, and grow our own food, and have a couple pigs, or some pulluus from Kiria for eggs. And a little girl." Amra finally looked up at that.

"What if I don't want a child? What if it's a boy?"

I shrugged. "Then just us, together."

"And what about Saart, and Bhon and Kamuli? If we invest so much into a shop, how can we pay them?"

"You know we can hear you." Amra's face darkened in a blush as Bhon's voice floated in the cabin, tinny and remote. I had forgotten to switch off the speaking tubes.

"They have a switch at the other end, too," I said into the air. Nosy interfering...

"We know," Saart said, and I sighed. The conversation was over, but Amra watched me for the rest of the ride.

We stopped on the other side of Kashidur City from the portal ground, the evening glow of the city overwhelming the stars. The taller buildings even blocked one of the rising moons.

There was a park we had used before, frequented by those with no permanent place of residence. We turned the transport into a 'U' shape to give us shelter. Tonight wouldn't be relaxing. We still had work to do.

Once we were set up, I found Kamuli Balion. The large woman seemed to know what I was thinking. She had the sample jar she had taken from the crate.

"There's more," I told her, and led her to my and Amra's bunk.

Kamuli had a small set of chemical reagents, a few beakers and testing vials, and a couple larger pieces of equipment including something she called a 'masseous spectrum-analyzer.' When we were in a friendly town, and she wasn't needed on guard duty, she would often help Saart with the coal mixture we fed to the engines, or cook up a few handy mixtures for when one of us encountered a local ailment we had not yet run across in our travels. None of us had expected to be able to catch the Lobath head-tentacle fever when we were on Loba, but the disease had proved surprisingly adaptable. Fortunately, Kamuli had been able to rework a local treatment into a reagent than worked for both Methiemum and Festuour.

Kamuli stared at the pile of jars on my bunk and then at me. "I will get my equipment," she said. "Meet me outside with these. I will need the campfire to help break down the pills into their components."

The others had finished setting up camp, and Saart had a healthy blaze going, seats from the transport placed around it, by the time Kamuli's equipment was set up—all polished metal rods and glass beakers. There were a few leather tubes and strangely shaped glass constructions, with a small pile of carefully labeled chemicals. I didn't know what the equipment did, only that it was among my doctor's prized possessions.

The sun set. We talked for several hours into the night while Kamuli worked. Saart made us a meal from whatever he had left lying around. I didn't taste it. I had shared my suspicion of the Baldek family's motives in sending medicine and we were all twitchy to discover Kamuli's results.

There was a gang of children who made their home in the bushes around the park. I'm sure they were thieves by day, but they came up to us openly as the night grew, their numbers larger than the last time we had been here.

Amra tsked. "There must be orphans from the Shudders epidemic joining them." She got up, gripping a change purse and reaching for the pot of Saart's stew. "They look like little crows, all skin and bones."

I didn't interfere, but I didn't help, while Amra doled out portions of stew and a small coin each for the urchins, her red wrap tucked in close. She had no problem helping others, but when it came to the uncertainty of raising one of her own, she balked.

Bhon held the pot as each child took a mouthful from Amra's ladle, and I tightened my jaw as each padam left her hand. I loved her generosity, even if I wanted to tear my hair out sometimes. Each of those children needed a good home, and a few coins wouldn't help that. I hoped the medicine in the delivery was clean. Maybe we could keep more orphans from joining this group.

After the children had departed to their leafy beds, the large doctor sat back with a sigh. Her headwrap was coming unpinned, though she didn't notice it. In the past few hours she had accumulated a pile of detritus around her—discarded jars and pills, samples of the crate packing material and even a small bit of the wood, and sheets of notes in her tight handwriting. Bhon had a cup of tea heated by the fire and brought it to her mate as she finished. Kamuli took a long draught of the hot liquid before she spoke.

"All of this medicine, despite which family

manufactured it," she began in her round tones, "is anti-seizing medication which will work to reduce the effects of the Shudders."

I felt my shoulders relax a little, until I saw she wasn't finished.

"Each family has a slightly different chemical concoction in their pill, likely a formula each family's scientists have discovered and not shared with the others. All of them include only the basic materials needed to assuage the fever." She felt around for one of the jars, inspecting the side in the firelight for the tiny maker's mark. "Except for these, from the Baldek family." My shoulders tightened again.

Kamuli held up one dark finger. "For a pregnant sufferer of the Shudders, when taking certain other medications commonly supplied by the Sureriaj, this pill can cause stillbirth. Specifically for Methiemum, it also has the ability to cause permanent sterility, if one takes multiple doses." Her brow was furrowed tighter than I had ever seen it on the normally placid woman. "I would never make this connection if I were not looking for something wrong with this medication. Given the fraction of the jars from the Baldek family and how they may be distributed on Methiem, I doubt any scientist will be able to discover this connection once the effects are realized."

"That's appalling." Amra stood, looking as if she would throw down her ever-present ledger. She looked to the bushes at the perimeter of the park. "I won't be any part to this."

"They can keep their dirty money, I say," Bhon added, incensed. "I ain't gonna be sterilized!"

I involuntarily looked at her choice of life mate. So did the others.

"I still have a choice!" she defended grumpily. "These crazy Sureri have got to be stopped. I say we take the price of this out of their ugly hides."

"But was it deliberate?" I asked. It could still be a manufacturing error. Vish let it be so. Even with all the other strange setbacks in customs.

Kamuli shook her head. "The additional compound could not be a simple accident. This was purposeful sabotage. My mate talks sense, even if she may not have as much at stake as she thinks." She threw an apologetic glance at Bhon, who bared her pointy teeth at Kamuli. "However, the only affected people would be those with the Shudders, who take a pill made by the Baldeks and who have not yet reproduced." She also spared a look for the bushes. "It may even help combat certain...ah, unfortunate social conditions."

Saart was as practical as always. "So can't we just deliver it and take the money?" He was leaning against a padded seat, his furry three-toed feet stretched out to the fire. "No, no. Stay with me." he explained, as everyone stared at him in shock. "There's a limited amount of medicine. The Baldek's tainted a fraction of the cargo, right? This stuff's only administered to certain people who have the Shudders, Kamuli tells us, and it *will* still cure them?" He waited for the doctor's slow nod. "Whatever the greasy gargoyles are planning, it can't be that effective. This sounds like a desperate plot by one family trying to lash out wherever they can. They'll hit the rare individual—probably less than the infant mortality rate. Deliver it, and get our money. Alert the officials later if you want."

When he explained it that way, it made sense. I could see the others considering it—even Bhon. The Baldek's plan didn't seem an effective strategy. I looked to Amra, who was still standing. The money from this delivery wouldn't be enough to buy a store, but if we didn't fulfill the contract, who knew how long until we climbed back out of debt? We would be traveling from homeworld to homeworld for cycles to come, until we were both old and gray.

Amra's face hardened, and I knew she was thinking the same thing. She opened her mouth. Perhaps the best thing was to deliver it anyway.

"Could the ingredients that make us sterile be added to other medicine?" she asked.

There was silence.

Kamuli bowed her head in thought, then picked up a few sheets of her notes. She spent a few minutes comparing her results.

"From my chromatography data, I would say...yes." There was shuffling around the campfire as the members of my crew shifted positions nervously. Slowly, Amra sat back down in her chair. She looked pale.

"I had not thought of this." The sheets trembled in Kamuli's hands, casting flickering shadows. "You are correct. The Baldek family could have—might have already—appended this concoction to almost every other medicine they are known to make, with little effect save some lessening of the potency. It would be just as difficult to find in other pills or reagents. They may be able to affect thousands of Methiemum families, over time."

Even Saart was frowning now.

Do the right thing. The Colonel's words came back to me. His strange promise. Had he sensed the contaminant in the pills? Had he heard of other shipments? It still didn't invalidate the money we needed from the delivery.

"Well, what are we supposed to do?" I asked my crew. "Go after the grand-dame who contracted me?" I didn't even know her true family, though I could guess. "Go after the entire Baldek family?" That was like trying to attack an entire government. Were they all in on it?

"We...could just tell the authorities in Kashidur City," Saart suggested, but his heart wasn't in it.

"And then these ruffians we're supposed to deliver to scatter like cockroaches under a light, and we still don't get our money," Bhon said. She hit one furry paw into her other palm with a meaty smack. "I want to take them down."

"This isn't a smuggling run," Amra put in, "it's a war, in all but name. Can we alert the maji?"

I thought about the flouncy woman who had been running the portal ground. "We can't trust this to someone else," I said. My heart was hammering, my mouth suddenly dry. "We have all the information here, now, with the contact waiting to receive their medicine in a few hours. Once the medicine is distributed, who's to say the pills will stay in their original jars? Each hospital might divide them up into different containers, all signs of the Baldek family erased." I cut the air with the side of my hand. "We have to deal with this delivery ourselves. Later we can bring in the authorities—" I nodded to Saart, "—and the maji." This time to Amra.

"And when we capture those bastards, then they will give us news on their employers," Kamuli said. There was a disturbing gleam in her eye.

We made plans, and got a few hours of fitful sleep before the sun rose.

PART THREE

The Delivery

- In the last five hundred cycles, more civil wars have been fought on the ten species' homeworlds than all the wars fought between species combined. I direct you to the census taken by adjunct to the Etanela Speaker recorded in 975 AAW. But have all wars truly been recorded? What defines a war taking place between planets separated by unknowable distances? I propose to the Assembly to study our histories for those wars never recorded, or hidden as 'trade disputes.' I think you will find much more conflict between the species than previously indicated.

Transcript of a section of a speech given to the Great Assembly of Species by Speaker Otuvari Thientect of Kiria, 982 AAW

The warehouse could have been a twin to the one on Sureri; similarly run down, dark windows shaded in the morning sunrise. No legitimate medical delivery would happen here.

I parked the transport in front, then sent Bhon around back to scout, her small form silent on her padded feet. Kamuli was with me, tucking her headwrap tight in anticipation. We made a show of checking the cargo to give Bhon time. I was sure there were eyes watching from the windows.

"We are not going to give them the medicine, yes?" Kamuli asked.

I shook my head. "I don't want these boxes to leave our hands, but we need proof of what the Baldeks are really doing."

Before long, Bhon returned, keeping to the shadow of the building. "I just about put my nose into it," she said, halfway out of breath from her jaunt. "I'm a frog if there ain't a whole herd of the hairy gargoyles out back, sitting around, playing cards and such. A couple new ones arrived while I watched. Looks like they put word out for reinforcements." She waved a furry paw to the dilapidated warehouse.

"Insurance if we've discovered their plan?" Saart asked.

"If they're even planning to pay us," I said. "We go in armed. Kamuli and Bhon in front, I'm in the middle, and Saart guards the rear. We need to capture at least one of them." I fixed my love with a steady stare. Her wrap was emerald green today, the bottom pinned up so she could move quickly. "We may need to leave this place in a hurry, and I need someone ready to pull the transport around if we come running with angry Sureriaj hot on our heels." I didn't say that this would keep her safe. She was not a trained fighter like Bhon and Kamuli. Neither were Saart and I, but we had been in our share of scraps.

Amra nodded, face serious. "Give those child killers what they deserve and get out quickly," she said.

Kamuli pushed the mold-encrusted doors open, her long knife at the ready. A mace and Bhon's crossbow hung low at her side. Bhon had both handcannons out. With their long reloading times, she would have to switch to a differently destructive weapon after a few rounds.

"Anyone here?" I called into the gloom. "We have cargo to deliver." I stopped behind a line of boxes and metal scrap. More piles lined shelves to either side. This warehouse was more crowded than the one on Sureri. High windows stained with dust let in limited light. A shape detached from the back of the warehouse, and came toward me.

She was Methiemum. My people.

The woman could have been from any of the cities on the southern continent. Three more men and a woman came forward to join her, just as unremarkable. All wore dark clothes, the better to disappear into unlit spaces.

Bhon raised her handcannons and Saart primed his contraption. What he held was technically a welder, or at least its ancestor was. What it did now—well, I wasn't completely sure. Kamuli was to my left, a little in front, her face stony.

I adjusted my plans.

"How much did they promise you for taking the medicine?" I asked. "Where are you taking it? To a hospital, or to some other dodgy warehouse?"

"You're not being paid to ask any questions," the woman in front growled. "And neither are we." She was large, with thick arms, probably from moving goods in warehouses like this. I saw hands drift to pockets, and put one of mine out to the side, palm down, to keep my crew from overreacting.

I held up my other hand, palm up, the broken pieces of the lock in it.

"But why would they need to secure ordinary medicine with one of these?"

The woman peered forward. "What is that?"

"An artifact prepared by a majus to lock the crates. How often have you seen one?"

The group looked at each other. A grumble came from the back. "I was only supposed to deliver a box, Wima. Weren't nothing said about the maji gettin' involved." The one who complained glanced over his shoulder, to the Sureriaj in back, no doubt. If I played this right, it might be nine of us against the Baldeks instead of four.

"I don't think your employers told you everything," I said, moving one step toward the woman in charge—Wima—hand still out in front. "Did they tell you which families the medicine came from? Did they tell you some of the pills could permanently ster—"

A report boomed in the warehouse, echoing around the large room.

Wima coughed. Red ran down her chin, and she slowly toppled forward. The others shouted, stepping away, and Bhon raised her guns, growling. My crew stepped back, nearer cover.

"I think that will be plenty o' yer rambling on," came another voice. Several Sureriaj stepped forward, guns at the ready. Their skin was pale, even in the dim light in the warehouse. He nodded sharply to his family members behind him, and there were four more loud gunshots.

My crew scattered as the bodies hit the ground. Kamuli and I dove behind a convenient stack of pallets, Bhon and Saart behind one of the taller shelves. Other reports followed, echoing in the large warehouse. Something whizzed and *thunked* into wood above me. I ducked, my gut tightening.

There was a silence. Reloading.

"Frente Yatulnath...or should I say *Baldek* Yatulnath?" I called from my hiding place.

"Eyah, yer've bodgered a right mess now, yer have," Yatulnath said. His head swiveled, trying to spot us. "Me employees donna need to know so much."

"They killed their delivery crew first," I whispered to Kamuli. "Why not us?"

"They would know too much of the Sureriaj soldiers," the large woman said. "Not enough guns for all, and we were the lesser threat."

"I have me familymates with me," Yatulnath called out. "Yer canna hide here. We will kill yer and take the cargo."

There was a burping cough from Saart's weapon. A line of flame disgorged from behind the shelves. Foreign curses sounded, and a lone shriek of pain. Good old Saart.

I peeked an eye around the corner of my pallet to see a Sureri rolling in the dirt, trying to beat out the flames on his clothing. A few of the others crept toward cover. I motioned to Kamuli, who had a knife up, tip held in one hand. The blade whizzed through the air and an alien clutched at his throat, sinking to his knees. The group moved faster, confused.

Two Sureriaj down, a whole bunch to go. I didn't like those odds.

Bhon's handcannons spoke, louder than the Sureriaj's small pistols. One shot went wild, but the other clipped a running Sureri in the shoulder, sending him spinning.

Behind cover, the aliens had time to finish reloading. More poured in from the back of the warehouse. Yatulnath, striding like a gruesome stork, gestured to either side, and his men spread out, flanking us.

I pulled a small pistol from my boot, and took a Sureri in the leg. He rolled, tripping one of his companions. I began reloading.

Answering fire. I ducked back, hoping the wooden pallets held. Kamuli loosed her crossbow, then hung it back on her belt. No time to crank it again. Another round of loud shots came from Bhon. Shadows flared as Saart flung gouts of flame, pushing the Sureriaj back.

There wasn't time to reload, and Saart couldn't keep them all away. I judged the distance to the door, the safety of the transport. Too far, out in the open. Doubtful any of us would reach the door.

"Run," I whispered to Kamuli. I hoped Saart and Bhon would see us and follow.

She nodded and faced the enemy.

I took one more look back, fumbling with my pistol—

With a shriek of tortured metal and shattering wood, the old war transport crashed through the front of the warehouse, sunlight bursting in behind it.

Splinters flew in all directions, and I fell back into the stack of pallets. A stake of wood buried itself in the ground between my feet. The transport rolled a few more feet into the warehouse, then lurched to a stop. The turrets Saart kept shiny and clean rotated to fix on the Sureriaj, and they cringed back. But when the transport's guns stayed silent—their ordnance long gone—the Baldeks grouped up, aiming their weapons at the new threat.

Projectiles began to clang off the metal sides of my transport with little effect. I gritted my teeth at the new dents, but the plating held. Amra was supposed to stay away from the fighting.

Before I could get up, a new sound, loud and thick, filled the air.

The transport bucked as the turret discharged a loud, glowing object over our heads and just behind the mass of Sureriaj. I covered my ears as the stack of pallets came down around me. The pressure of the blast dug into my skin. My sight went dark for a moment.

When I could see again, I peered dazedly into what was left of the Baldek troops, my ears ringing. A long-fingered Sureri hand twitched by itself. A leg, with no body. Blood. Worse. I swallowed bile, saw Saart prone, on the floor, blood around his leg. Bhon was holding a hand to her side, trying to drag him back to cover.

Kamuli must have been protected by the pallet. She bounded forward, mace up, and caved in the skull of the nearest Sureriaj. I yelled at her, though I couldn't hear myself. We needed one alive. My ears were ringing, noises indistinct. I stumbled to the left.

Staggering around the broken pallets, I went directly to the long-legged form of Yatulnath, barely upright. The mass of aliens in the back had caught the worst of the blast, shielding the others with their bodies. I caught him as I lurched past, swinging him around to rest between me and the three last Sureriaj standing.

"Don't try anything!" I shouted to them, and raised my pistol to Yatulnath's head. I needn't have bothered. The others were stunned, eyes blank. Even Yatulnath took a moment to respond, before calling to his family members to stand down. As they did, Kamuli and Bhon limped out to cover them. We were covered with tiny burns and scratches. Bhon had Saart's flamethrower, and my old friend was still lying motionless, glasses thrown to one side and cracked. Unconscious, or worse? I couldn't spare the time to check. Thanks to Amra, and whatever she made the transport do, we had the advantage. Good thing she at least was out of harm's way, behind the metal walls of the transport.

I needed information. "What's your plan?" I shouted to Yatulnath, and poked him in the head with my pistol. I hoped he didn't know it was unloaded. Sounds were starting to come back to me, but he only hunched his narrow shoulders.

"I haven't got much patience at this point," I said loudly, looking into his face so he could see my words. "Are those your cousins?" I thrust my chin toward the other Sureriaj, hands at their sides and guns on the floor.

"Two cousins. One brother," Yatulnath said. I could barely hear him, but I caught his meaning.

"Bhon?" I gestured to my most bloodthirsty body-guard in case she was as deaf as me.

There is little love lost between the Festuour and the Sureriaj. Bhon almost leapt forward, raising the flamethrower to one of the captives.

"Shall I guess which is the brother?" I asked, and Yatulnath shuddered under me. Siblings were precious to them, even more than to Methiemum. They would gladly, eagerly, betray extended family for those closer to them.

The Sureri in the middle reached out with one thin hand, toward his sibling. Bhon shifted the glowing tip of the flamethrower to him.

Yatulnath began to speak.

"There will be more comin'," he said. "Yer canna stop this by killin' me or me brother. Shipments are goin' out all over yer planet."

"We'll deal with that," I told him. "Why are you try-ing to sterilize us?" I moved around to face the Sureri, still holding my gun up.

He grimaced as he saw me, his eyes gone cold as if he watched a poisonous insect. "We Baldek know what's really happenin'," he spit. "Other Sureriaj great families are weak. They let the Methiemum stay on our planet. Yer kind are the worst. See something, and yer take it. For ages, we barred the other species from our home, but yer and yer kind forced yer way in. The other spe-cies too, but yer are the worst. Yer breed like maggots, eyah? Just because me own don't grow so fast, yer think yer can take our own planet away from us!"

"That's insane. Why would we want to live there?"

"Eyah, so yer ask, but we know better." Yatulnath

said. "Yer have people living on all the ten homeworlds. It's only a smidge o' time until yer start breeding like yer always do."

"Those are trading posts," I told him. "Those are so we can *trade* with you. Both of us win." I glanced at Bhon and Kamuli. They looked as confused as I was. I snuck a peek at Saart, still out. I wondered why Amra didn't come out to help him.

"That's how it starts, eyah," Yatulnath returned. "But the Baldek will keep yer kind from takin' over all of the ten homeworlds by stoppin' yer incessant breedin'. See if we won't!"

He surged to his feet, pushing my gun away from his head, and shouting orders in the Sureri language. His family members dove for their weapons.

Bhon shot a blast of flame at one and Kamuli blocked another, stabbing with her knife. Yatulnath's brother raised his gun and fired. Kamuli grunted, staggering off balance, holding her arm. She recovered quickly, punching her attacker, her left bicep showing a gash of red. As he reeled back, she hit him with the butt of her mace. The Baldek dropped.

But Yatulnath reached a dead alien, grasping the dropped firearm.

"Stop!" I cried, and he froze. "We can fix this!"

Yatulnath snarled wordlessly, and raised his weapon.

Bhon's blast of flame caught him full on, turning him into a torch. But before the blazing form fell, his gun fired, and something slammed into my shoulder. I staggered, tripped, and the world tilted.

* * *

Kamuli's dark face swam into view.

"How long?" I muttered.

"It was only a minute or two. You hit your head when you fell."

I tried to raise my left hand to feel my head and pain shot through my arm, overriding my massive headache.

"And you were shot, of course. You will need a hospital."

"Thanks." I grimaced. There was a cloth bandage wrapped around my upper arm, stained a blotchy red.

My mind replayed the last several seconds of the confrontation.

"Saart?" I gently pulled my head up to look around. The warehouse was lit by the dying light of the Sureri bonfire, the sunlight coming through the broken doors. It stank of fried flesh and spilt blood and I forced my stomach back down. Yatulnath's brother was trussed by the pallets, unconscious.

I caught sight of my Festuour chef and mechanic off to the side. He was sitting up, peering through his cracked glasses and pressing a matted bloody paw into his thigh. Bhon was ripping up a sheet of fabric beside him.

"It's fine," Saart grated, pinning me with his brilliant blue eyes. "Shrapnel nipped my leg. I'll be dandy in a few days." From his heavy panting and the amount of blood, I wasn't sure. I could see shredded flesh beneath his paw.

We were all accounted for, and mostly whole. We didn't have our money, but maybe, with our captive—

I looked around again, carefully. Two Festuour, one large Methiemum woman. I would have expected Amra to be out of the transport as soon as the fight was over, her wrap pulled around her, making sure everyone was alright.

I pulled myself to my feet. The other two were busy with Saart. I walked as fast as I could to the transport, wincing and cursing, holding my arm, and tried not to scream as I jerked the hatch open. I clambered clumsily inside.

Amra gazed at me, face tight, one hand over her abdomen. A crimson puddle was pooling beneath her. My head swiveled to the tank's windshield, where I saw the tiny hole the stray bullet had made.

"Kamuli!" I called. She was there in a moment at the panic in my voice, and bent over my accountant...my love.

"This is not good," she said quietly. Amra had closed her eyes, but I thought she still heard us.

"But you can help her."

"I...do not know," she replied. "This is worse than Saart."

"We're in a transport full of medical supplies, for Vish's sake! Find something! And get the others in here!" I pushed at her with my good arm and Kamuli leapt back out the hatch.

"Keep pressure on it!" she called.

Amra's eyes opened, a rictus of pain on her face.

"Don't worry," I told her. "Kamuli will take good care of you. She'll make sure—"

"Did you have any idea...what you were do-ing...attacking a troop of Baldek...soldiers?" she gasped, interrupting me. "Lucky I was here to...to rescue you."

"I'm sorry," I said, my voice a whisper. I tried to figure out where to press. How not to hurt her more.

"We'll never get the...money now," she said. "If you...plan our marriage like this, I'll shoot you...myself."

I looked down. There would be a wedding. I hadn't realized before how much I wanted one. I wanted to marry this woman, have children with her, and have our own little business on Methiem, selling trinkets from around the ten homeworlds.

"You will marry me, won't you?"

"Of course, you idiot," she grated. "Talk to me. Keep me awake."

Behind her, the base of the turret was still turned into the warehouse.

"How did you fire it?" I placed one hand on hers, shaking and white over her stomach. Crimson stood bold against her green wrap. She was too warm, feverish and weak. I helped her hold pressure on the wound. One hand I put on hers, the other I slid around her back, trying to keep my face calm at her cries of pain.

"The Colonel gave me...one casing before he left," Amra told me between gasps. Red seeped through her fingers as she spoke. It stained my hand too, hot and sticky. I couldn't feel any blood behind her. The bullet was still inside. "Old. Might not work. Said it was what the tank was built...to use. Couldn't...depend on it...working."

"So you didn't tell me about it. Not a sure strategy." Her accounting side, letting me plan for the worst case. My jaw tensed. "And he said he wouldn't get involved. Meddling maji." Otherwise we would all be dead. "It must use ordnance made by the maji of the House of Potential. No wonder these things aren't used any more. With a cost like that, you could never fund them." With this cost. I kissed Amra's forehead.

"The Sureriaj?" she asked.

"You got them. We left one alive to question. I need to find another buyer for our cargo, with the Baldek's portion removed. Even without this contract, we can turn a profit. People with the Shudders still need medicine. Then we can get married. Just—"

"Just a few more jobs...right?" my fiancé guessed.

Kamuli, sweating, with scratches on her arms, pushed through the hatch.

"I have painkillers, but the cargo section is a mess. The Colonel only opened the one crate. Ramming the building and firing the turret turned the jars to shards of glass."

She held out a handful of pills, some of her own making, and some from the delivery.

"The Shudders medicine? Will it help her?" I tried to get a better look but Amra grunted in pain and I kept my position.

"It will reduce inflammation and stabilize her metabolism until we get to the hospital. But..."

I counted the handful of little gray things in her hand. "You don't know which jar they came from."

Kamuli shook her head. "It is more than likely not the contaminated medicine."

I looked at Amra. "Are you sure she can't make it without—"

Amra's eyes tightened and she winced.

"She is losing too much blood," Kamuli said. "We will need to dose Saart as well."

"Do it," Amra croaked.

"Do it," I agreed. We'd sort things out later. We couldn't waste any more time.

"No more deliveries," she whispered. Kamuli shooed me out of the way to tend to Amra herself. We traded positions gingerly.

"No more deliveries," I agreed. I didn't have to think hard about it.

"Help me lay her down, get the others ready," Kamuli told me. "On three." Amra screamed when we moved her and my heart almost stopped in my chest.

I helped Bhon drag Saart and the last unconscious Sureri to the passenger section, then jumped into the pilot's seat, still slick with my fiancé's blood.

We left the bodies where they lay. Bhon stoked the engines and I drove full speed down narrow streets.

* * *

Kashidur City is the largest trading port on Methiemum, and the capital city of the largest nation. One of the best medical facilities was not ten minutes distant, the way the cargo transport rumbles. The promise of medicine for the Shudders got us in quickly.

Saart and Amra were wheeled into the operating theater on stretchers. Kamuli came in as our personal doctor and Bhon came with her mate. All of us bore injuries to a degree.

As was the custom, the theater was open to observers and students of the medical arts, behind a line of glass windows. This early in the morning, the seats were empty, except for one person.

"What's *he* doing here?" The old majus was calmly sitting in a corner. I sucked in air as a masked nurse with her gray hair in a bun slid a needle into my arm. It started to go numb and I let out a breath.

"Thought you might need help wrapping things up," the Colonel shouted through the glass. I could barely hear him. "Those crates are still sealed, if I remember right."

"But how did he get here before us?" I asked a masked Kamuli, who was helping the nurse. Amra had a small crowd of people around her, and medicines and poultices vanished into the group. Saart had his own crowd, examining his leg. Kamuli ignored me.

Time passed, as it does in hospitals. They even

forced Bhon down at one point to treat her burns and cracked ribs.

They told us Saart would lose the leg. The damage was too great, too much of a risk to his life. Saart was stoic; I complained more than he did. The amputation was quick, Saart rendered unconscious by a mask of ether. The first thing he did when awoke was to ask for pen and paper to begin designing a prosthetic leg. And new glasses.

On Amra, we heard nothing definite. Doctors traded places, a steady stream of medicines arrived.

I must have been dozing, seated in an out-of-the-way chair, and woke to the theater door opening. A woman with olive skin and a long black braid entered, mask down around her neck. A white smock covered her, but I thought she was wearing a formal white dress underneath. Was she another doctor? She immediately went to the majus in the observation nook, a white bell tied to the very end of her braid chiming as she walked.

"Where have you been hiding?" she called through the window. The old majus had the grace to look embarrassed. "No matter. Deal with you later."

She looked around, and settled on me. I stared groggily back. The painkillers were affecting me.

"You're the one with the illegal medicines and the Sureriaj prisoner."

I almost answered her before I realized she hadn't asked. I propped myself up on my good arm and glared back from my chair, taking a moment to check Amra. She was sleeping, her chest slowly raising and lowering under a thin sheet. There was blood on it. "Who are you?"

"The one asking the questions." Her dark brows drew down. "The maji have an interest in how these medicines and the Baldek came to be here." Of course she was a majus. How could I have missed that haughty stare?

"You are of the House of Healing?" Kamuli asked. She had only just sat down, a dressing around her upper arm and headwrap near to falling off. "Can you help?" She pointed to Amra.

"I am House of Healing, but not that kind," The woman answered. She tapped her head. "I deal with this." Her glance swept the room, registering our faces, and she frowned. "But I'll see if I can do anything."

She walked to Amra, and stretched both hands out over her. Her head tilted to one side, as if she heard birdsong, or a sound the rest of us couldn't. For a silent minute, her hands roamed above Amra's body. Then she picked up a jar of medicine beside the operating table, investigating each one in turn. Finally, she faced us.

"The good news is that Doctor Chaptali did an excellent job," she said. "There is much internal damage, but I believe she will recover, in time." The majus picked up one of the bottles of liquid on the table. "The bad news is that I must apologize for the contamination in these vials. I don't know what happened to them."

"What contamination?" Kamuli asked, but my stomach was clenching. I knew the answer.

"A foreign compound, not supposed to be there. The poison is in her reproductive system already, reacting with the antibiotics."

I closed my eyes for a moment, then looked to Kamuli, her head in her hands. Either she guessed the wrong pills or Amra got contaminated medicine from the hospital. We would never know, and in either case, this was exactly the Baldeks' plan. We should have avoided the warehouse and gone to the maji to begin with.

"You can't...?" I gestured vaguely with my good hand.

The majus gave me an apologetic look. "She is still very weak. Any part of her biology I changed now would kill her."

"I hoped..."

"I'm very sorry, but," she scanned the room once more, "if everyone is out of immediate danger..." Doctor Chaptali, slumped in the background, signaled his agreement. "I'd like to discuss what to do with the crates and the prisoner sitting outside this hospital."

"You can have the Baldek, but the crates are my property, until they get delivered." My eyes went back to Amra. Bhon watched me, her face pained.

The woman tapped her hand on her leg, impatient. "They're your property...for now. Only because I am choosing not to confiscate the entire lot." She fixed me with her dark-eyed gaze again, and I blinked first. This woman had *hard* eyes. "Despite the question of who owns them, what are we to do with illegally imported medicines containing compounds causing sterility in Methiemum?"

I realized my mouth was open, and hastily closed it. How did she know?

"Not a healer. Still from the House of Healing." The majus wiggled her fingers by way of explanation. "The biological contaminants in the melody of the medicine are very similar to what I heard in this bottle." She lifted the vial used on Amra.

I narrowed my eyes. "Melody?"

"Never mind." She wiped the air with a flat hand. "The cargo?"

"I have a lot of expense in that manifest. Even more now." I glanced at Amra. "Plus, I'm recently out of work, and...saving up for a wedding."

The majus pursed her lips. "You're not the only one with expenses. We'll have to bring in maji and scientists to check all medical supplies recently imported to Methiem." Something relaxed in my chest. Others knew. Even if we did nothing, this...this majus would take care of it. It wasn't just us anymore.

"I have a thought," volunteered an old and scratchy voice. We both looked to the Colonel, as he entered the main theater.

"What if you turn this whole thing back on its ear? Keep the good stuff, and send our 'extra' poisoned medicine back to those who made it in the first place."

The younger majus looked thoughtful.

"Would they even use it? Would it have the same effect on the Sureriaj?" I asked.

"Not as much," she answered, "though that's not the point."

"Could you make the whole Baldek family die out?" I asked. For Amra. For those new orphans in the park.

The female majus shook her head. "No. Some Baldeks might end up taking their own medicine, but I will not continue this war." She contemplated a moment. "I *will* make them recognize their own handiwork. Show them we know. Teach them this is not the way of the Great Assembly. Our way is peace. Otherwise, one errant faction can give an entire species a bad name."

Her words made me look to my fiancé again. My vision of a little shop with children in the yard was fading.

"I think the Naiyul constables were investigating the Baldeks," Kamuli said, her eyes red. I remembered our tails on Sureri. "They may be able to help."

"But can they help enough?" I asked. "This took the influence of an entire *family* of the Sureriaj. Surely the

Methiemum provinces are busy dealing with the Shudders epidemic?"

The woman smiled back, thin-lipped and nasty. "There are ways. The Council has the influence and finance."

"The Council of the Maji?" My eyes widened. This woman had connections. The Council answered only to the senatorial power of the Great Assembly. Here was a power that could rival that of an entire family of the Sureriaj—that of a multi-species senate with power bases on all ten homeworlds.

My eyes strayed back to Amra.

"You can't just take the cargo," I said quietly. "I have to make sure she's safe." My stomach clenched at the emptiness of my threat. One man against the entire Great Assembly. This one majus could incapacitate me by herself.

She followed my gaze and gave me another smile, this one understanding. "I think we can come to an arrangement."

"Which is?" Would they simply throw us all in prison? I still didn't trust the maji.

"For the services rendered in discovering what might have become an interspecies war, the Council can send a reward your way. With the other cleanup we'll have to do, a little more expense won't be noticed." That got our attention.

The majus named a price. My mouth dropped open.

It was enough to keep Amra and I comfortable for many cycles, as well as Bhon and Kamuli. Saart would have enough left over to tinker with whatever old gadgets he liked, build a dozen steam-powered mechanical legs. Our little store was a reality. As many children as...except not.

The silence stretched out.

The Majus was waiting. I offered my good hand to shake. "It's a deal."

As we shook, she was already talking. "With the samples here, we can start a full-scale search for the rest of the contaminated medicine. We'll turn this back on the Baldeks in no time. And I'll have your payment drawn up officially as soon as I get back to the Council."

I froze. She didn't just know the Council, she was *on* it. This was the head of the House of Healing herself. If anyone could stop the Baldeks in their genocide, this woman could. Maybe the maji were not only out for themselves. The two here had shown honor in dealing with a small-time merchant.

Sometime later, I leaned over Amra as her eyes fluttered open.

"How would you like to have a place right here in Kashidur City?" I asked.

She grasped my hand, weakly. "Prot. We don't have—"

"We have everything we need," I told her. "And I have you." I took a deep breath. "After the wedding, what do you think about adopting a little girl? I've been told there are a lot of orphans, victims from the Shudders epidemic."

Amra looked back, confused, and I smiled at her. "It's an idea. You don't have to decide now. Rest up. We have a lot to plan." I would break the news—all the news—when she was a little better. I looked to Saart, Kamuli, and Bhon. No more deliveries.

The First Majus in Space

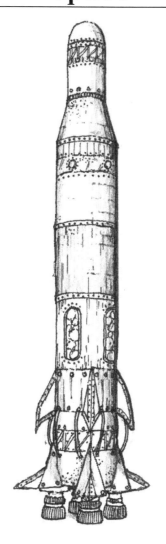

First Flight of the *Vimana Aryuman*

- The Houses of the Maji are vastly different in scope, yet none are considered above the others. Each has a balance for the other five. The House of Healing may undo the House of Communication's change, one from the House of Strength could stand firm against the draw of the House of Potential, and the House of Grace can evade the House of Power's raw might.

Fragment of a parchment, dated circa 550 B.A.W.

Origon pushed through the multitudes packing the arena on the outskirts of Kashidur City. A great shrouded hulk loomed in the distance at the far end of the crowded space, big as a building. If he remembered correctly, this used to be a forest at the edge of the city. The plain was flat compacted dirt now, soon to be baked earth, if the hot and sunny weather held. Odd to place a lone construction out here, then pack people around it. Methiem was already the most populous of the ten homeworlds, and members of other species had been arriving all morning at the portal ground from their own far-flung worlds or from the Nether.

Excited babble assaulted him on all sides, and air currents carried their intent in the trills of the Symphony of Communication.

"Look there, mama!" A child Lobath, her head tails not yet long enough to braid.

"They told me it was bigger than a building. They weren't lying." Two Festuour in conversation.

"What does it do? Why now?"

"How much did you spend on that?"

He could hear tension of alien species in the music, wondering at the presumption of the Methiemum. This latest proof of their technological arrogance grated on the slower and more cautious species. He was not so bothered. The trader species made a lot of interesting gadgets.

"Get yer fried keilbash!"

Origon's feathery crest ruffled as a hawker jostled past him with a tray of sausages that smelled over-cooked and over seasoned. No sense killing it and wasting the meat with all that spice. Belatedly, he moved a long-fingered hand over the inside pocket of his colorful robe where he kept his coins. No one would dare steal from a majus, but in this crowd, a cutpurse might not even realize from whom he was stealing.

As he shoved closer, smoothing his moustache down, he eyed the structure at the front of the crowd, sur-rounded by ladders and scaffolding. The canny Methiemum had an open invitation to anyone and eve-ryone to watch the unveiling of their grand invention. If they could have made a profit from it, they might have called the ten species here to reveal a giant block of cheese, but he didn't think that was the case. The thing was the presentation, and the Methiemum were masters of it.

He thrust forward, using his height and sharp elbows to create paths, and ignoring curses thrown his way.

"Oy! Watch yer bony arms, ye great robed buffoon!" The angry Sureri, like a furry, starved gargoyle sans wings, layered doubts upon his parentage, his furry face screwed up into a grimace. There were always those who were jealous.

Origon paid him no mind. The maji who attended should have prominent positions, and he was no exception. He finally reached the front of the arena, where a line of the Mayoral Guard stood at attention. The soldiers parted at a glare from him, recognizing him as a majus from the badge with his house colors, and Origon took a place by other important people—including at least one Etanela Speaker, half again as tall as he.

"Greetings, Majus," the Speaker said, her long fingers making a graceful curve through the air. From high above, her large pale eyes acknowledged him from a face surrounded by a mane of light hair.

"Speaker," he returned the greeting, settling beside her.

Beings of every shape and size stretched to his right and left, pushing each other, trying to get closer to the front, though the line of guards held them back. They were before a raised stage, the Methiemum's shrouded construct towering overhead. It cast a shadow across the crowd, now reaching back to the edges of the area. The dirt plain, stretching nearly as far as he could see, was even fuller than when he arrived.

A snap of material drew Origon's attention. With a cheer from the crowd, the immense sheet covering the structure dropped, folding in on itself. There was a round of gasps, and an immediate buzz of conversation. He barely suppressed his reaction, forcing his crest to lay flat. No need to look completely ignorant. He had been consulted—indirectly—on how wind currents would affect a smooth object at a great height. He was prepared for some sort of great balloon, perhaps launched from the top of a building, but this was...impressive.

It shone in the sunlight, bright enough to make him squint. The main structure was a cylinder of burnished metal, sleek and bright, rounding to a dome far overhead. The base and jutting fins were sparsely ornamented, as was the main shaft, but the filigree and hatching he could see was finely done. It looked like nothing so much as a giant finger, pointing to the sky. People were shielding their eyes, gesturing to the gleaming object.

One of the official-looking Methiemum on the platform spoke from behind a podium. Origon thought it was the mayor of the province of Kashidur, though he could hardly keep such people straight. The man's voice was amplified by a tube glowing with stored energy of the Houses of Communication and Potential.

"Welcome, all!" The man shaded his eyes with a hand. "I see people from every homeworld of the Great Assembly of Species here today. Good, good." The man swept a hand to the great structure behind him. "The capsule you see before you will shortly begin a monumental journey." There were exclamations, and questions from the crowd, asking how such a thing could move.

But the mayor was still speaking. "It will bring a crew of Methiemum, and one of our revered maji, up to our moon, Ksupara." The closest and smallest of Methiem's three satellites. Better to start small, if such a plan was to be believed.

"Once there, the crew will explore the new land, mapping and providing the first scientific study of Ksupara." To see what minerals were available, Origon mentally translated. The audience shouted and muttered at this pronouncement. Others had come to the same conclusion. Why waste so many resources to build this thing, when the ten homeworlds were connected by portals, an easy step from one place to another? Leave it to the Methiemum to want more than one homeworld.

The mayor continued his speech, detailing how the majus would assist flying the shuttle, establish the coordinates of a new portal ground, and bring the crew back from Ksupara 'the short way.' Origon of course knew all this. If maji could simply make a portal anywhere, he would have traveled over much more of the universe. Sadly, one could only make a portal where one had been before, thus the capsule. Otherwise, every species might have ventured to their moons and to other planets in their solar system.

While the mayor rambled on, telling of the construction and planning required, Origon examined the capsule. A majus was required to fly it, as in all great acts, but as far as he could tell, the vehicle was fashioned wholly by hand, and not by maji changing the Symphony. He marveled at how much wealth the Methiemum tied up in this mechanical venture. No wonder they invited everyone to see. They could at least make some of their money back with the increased trade. The Methiemum, after all, practiced usury with abandon, which no self-respecting Kirian would do.

As the mayor spoke, a group of people climbed a tall ladder behind him, connected to a walkway at the top of the structure. They reached the top when the mayor wound up his speech. "So we see the prowess of the Methiemum. Our species reaches out to the nine others, showing, and soon sharing, what heights can be achieved by the sweat of our hands. Without even the assistance of the maji, we have built this vehicle you see behind me." He gestured backwards again. "It will be the first to travel between the stars, built by the technology and ingenuity of my people. And thus, I set this great craft, the *Vimana Aryuman*, in motion, lighting the fuse to allow its passage to Ksupara." The mayor stooped around his prominent belly and pressed a button.

With a *whoosh*, flames banked around the capsule behind the stage, slowly building higher, to the appreciative cries of the audience.

It was a show for the gullible crowds. Origon could hear the Symphony of Power's strident chords deep in the melody of the shuttle. The visible flames were just a coal-fired pilot light to a great furnace stored in the belly of the capsule.

So why is it that I am standing down here in the crowd?

He was one of the best suited for this purpose, his abilities rare even among the ranks of the maji. Very few could hear the Symphony of two houses; only three other maji were members of both the House of Communication and of the House of Power. For this capsule to fly to Ksupara, a majus would be needed to control the fuel burn with the House of Power, as well as correct the shuttle's flight through the air with the House of Communication. He supposed two maji could try to coordinate their changes to the Symphony, but it would be much harder than one majus controlling both. The mayor only mentioned having one. Thus the capsule required the rare majus who could hear both Symphonies at once to function at peak efficiency. Like him. Yet no one had asked him. He squinted up at the walkway looking for which majus had been chosen in his place.

One of the figures, vaguely familiar, waved from the walkway near the top of the capsule. There were only a few thousand maji total, so many were known on sight, even to the common folk. What was his name? The mayor was speaking again, announcing the titles and names of the crew. Origon ignored the others until the mayor got to...ah. Teju. Origon had to admit the boy was a fitting choice. Teju was the one Methiemum out of the four maji in existence with access to the Houses of both Communication and Power. However, he was recently raised from the ranks of the apprentices, if Origon remembered correctly. A fitting choice, perhaps, but not a strong one.

The pretty show flames licked the bottom of the giant cylinder. The crew would be on their way shortly, the great capsule lifting high into the air. Just one more opportunity passing him by, given to a majus by far his inferior.

The air cracked overhead, and Teju stiffened. Shouts grew in the audience, arms rose, pointing. The line of guards pushed forward. Origon swung around, searching. A glint of reflected sunlight caught his eye, but the giant Etanela next to him motioned, and her elbow caught his head and knocked him sideways. Origon scanned the arena, trying to get his bearings. He rubbed his temple.

"My apologies," the Etanela Speaker said, stooping. "What do you see? What happened?"

Origon ignored her. *There.* A cloaked person, all in gray-green, wearing a wide-brimmed hat, surely sweltering in the hot Kashidur sunlight. Something flashed again, a reflection from a long metal tube, peeking out underneath the long overcoat. A projectile weapon of some sort?

Origon thrust ahead, aiming for the figure. "Move!" he called to those in front of him. They surged, not listening. He knew he was too late even as he fought the crowd. The cloaked figure raised the long metal cylinder to its face for a second shot, and Origon let the

Symphony of Communication flow around him, catching chords representing air currents as they flashed by. He used his song to tune the chords, harmonizing, arranging them in a lattice. Crystalline yellow, the color of the House of Communication, outlined a tunnel before him. His alteration to the music shifted the air, magnifying his vision.

Origon got a brief glance of fine hair covering a gruesome face, a flash of an eye and thin, high cheek. Then the head jerked out of his tunnel vision by the gun's recoil. It was enough to recognize one of the Sureriaj, possibly even the one who had accosted him earlier. The xenophobic species was outspoken, but a rare sight on other homeworlds.

Belatedly, Origon grabbed at the notes of the bullet's course, but it was far too fast, the beat frenetic, and the notes of its music slipped from him. The bullet pinged off the walkway to the capsule. It was not right that a tube with powder in it could defeat a majus.

"May all your feathers fall out!" He cursed the shooter. The saying might not apply outside his species, but he felt better for it. Still, some attribute of the Sureri nagged at him. Eye color? Were brown eyes common? He thought most Sureriaj were orange or gray-eyed, depending on the family lineage. And the eyes looked too small. Large eyes in a gargoyle face made Sureriaj generally unattractive to the other species.

Yet another shot rang out. The Mayoral Guard were hopelessly bogged down, unable to get to the shooter. The crowd heaved against him and Origon held on to a railing to keep his balance. Three shots. If he was incredibly fast, the shooter might have reloaded between the first and second shot, but a third, so close? There must be another barrel to his rifle, or he had a second one, already loaded. This was no snap decision to sabotage.

He followed the path of the bullets, feeling the way they cut through the melody of the air, and saw Teju slumped against the rail of the walkway. A pit of fire rose in Origon's stomach. How dare someone shoot one of the maji!

When he looked back, the shooter was gone. Someone jostled him, then he was buffeted by dozens of people running. Clothing of all colors and beings of all sizes whipped past his view, blocking any hope of seeing where the shooter went.

"Ancestor's eggs," Origon cursed, and began running against the panicked crowd, back to the stage. He wrapped his robe close around his legs to keep it from getting stepped on. If he were high on the walkway, he might be able to see where the shooter was going. And he could help Teju.

It took longer than it should have to push through the crowd. Halfway through, he gave up and extended a hand. He caught at notes, readying his song to make a windy corridor. The air resisted, and Origon cursed again. The Symphony could not be changed in the same way twice in the same place and time. This was too similar to his magnifying glass.

He sighed, listening instead for the jangling chords of the Symphony of Power. They were harder to hear, discordant and irregular. People's connections in a crowd were not so easy to change as the wind. Orange light dripped from his fingers as he encouraged those in front of him to notice his importance and move aside. He ran through.

When Origon reached the stage, he reversed the change he made to the Symphony of Power and regained the rest of his song. Every person was defined by their own specific vibration. Invest enough of that song permanently in changes and what would be left?

Rilan was waiting for him, plucking and fiddling with one of the white corseted dresses she was forced to wear on official business. It set off her black hair and dark features. She was here as representative of the Council of the Maji, then. He wasn't surprised. Nor was he surprised she arrived before him. *She* had probably been invited to sit with the officials, being Methiemum herself. He nodded to her curtly and they both strode to the ladder leading to the walkway.

"Don't know if he'll survive," Rilan said, as if it hadn't been two cycles since they last spoke, this time. "The shooter was good."

"Teju is the only one here trained to set the shuttle on its way," Origon remarked casually. He shifted his eyes enough to see Rilan's wry expression. He had missed her. Had they truly known each other for more than twenty cycles?

"There's a good reason why you weren't chosen, Ori," she replied. "We all know you're one of the best at manipulating the Houses of Power and Communication when they're together. But you aren't Methiemum. The government was insistent."

"Teju is little more than a child. Now look what has happened," Origon remarked. If he had been up there, he could have deflected those bullets.

"And what if we had chosen you?" Rilan continued. "You'd be up there chewing those Sureriaj bullets right now."

Origon snorted, but ignored the jab. "You think it is their species as well?"

"Sure. Who else has trained marksmen who can hit a target that far away? Most people would miss their own foot with one of those things."

"Agreed," Origon said. Guns had only been around for fifty or sixty cycles, one of the nastier inventions of the Methiemum. The Sureriaj favored the weapons, though they had grudgingly accepted the invention at first. Most other beings still used swords and staves, trusty things with no need to reload, or crossbows for range. Origon wondered if that was where the idea for the capsule originated. It was in essence a giant gun, shooting at the ground, from what he could tell.

"In any case, that's the rumor from people who saw the shooter firsthand." Rilan added. "One of the cabinet members passed it on to me."

Another reason to be included with the important people. Origon opened his mouth to say he had seen the shooter firsthand as well, but stopped. Rilan would ask for more details and he honestly did not have any except for brown eyes. He was beginning to doubt himself on that account. Later.

They reached the ladder and began climbing. Origon kept the Symphony uppermost in his mind, listening to the notes and phrases of the complex construct flash by as they rose above the milling crowds. The Symphony of Power's glissandos and trills mirrored the holes and directions of the people below, many of them still running. The Symphony defined everything. What he saw was just the physical manifestation of it. The other four Symphonies were there too, but of course he couldn't hear them.

"Can you give us a shield?" Rilan called down to him. He shook his head, then realized she wasn't looking.

"Not now. We will not be able to reach Teju."

Once created, the underlying vibration would resist him creating a second shield until he was far away from this spot or much time had passed. He would have to hold it constant—unable to interact with Teju and the crew —or let it drop and be more or less defenseless.

Only now he felt just as defenseless, climbing the multiple-story ladder.

A few minutes later, they reached the top, without getting shot at. Up here the air currents were fresher, Communication's melody almost playful.

Rilan hurried forward to Teju, who seemed to be the only one injured. One of the crew, probably the doctor, was already there.

"Here, Councilor," the doctor said to Rilan. She crouched over the fallen man and pressed her hands to his abdomen, where blood ran freely. Origon saw the white and olive green glow form around her hands, sinking into the injured Teju's belly. He always thought olive was a strange secondary color to complement the white of the House of Healing, but then, one did not choose the secondary color—it grew naturally. He was secretly happy for the anonymity of having two house colors—yellow for Communication and orange for Power. It meant he had no secondary color.

"Shiv's toenails!" Rilan cursed at Teju. "Hold still! I'm a psychiatrist, not a surgeon. I'll do what I can, but you can't go dying on me." Origon saw the crimson flow lessen slightly, and the bewhiskered doctor pressed a cloth to the wound, but there was an awful lot of blood darkening the narrow walkway. Rilan had never been good at physically healing with the Symphony, but then, not many maji were.

"Is anyone else injured?" he asked the shaken crew, cowering on the carpeted walk. The whole thing trembled with the smallest breath of wind, and Origon was tempted to stabilize it, but that would take too much effort and time. He asked in the Trader's Tongue, the common form of communication between species. He and Rilan had not needed to use it, of course, being maji.

"No, Majus," answered one of them, an older woman with gray hair pulled into a severe bun. She looked only slightly less petrified than the rest. She and the rest of the crew were wearing matching heavy blue suits with gray piping, thick and all one piece.

After a moment's contemplation, Origon knelt down, too, behind the engraved metal handrail. He wouldn't be able to see as far, but he was taller than the average Methiemum and didn't want his topfeathers shaved off by another bullet.

"Did you see the shooter?" a crewmember asked.

Origon nodded. "From very close. It was to be one of the Sureriaj. Now quiet, while I find him again." He listened to notes from the House of Power, peering over the walkway's handrail. Far below, he heard trills of fear running through the crowd. There was a strange base line as well, which he ignored. The Symphony was as complex as reality and often more confusing. Origon traced the path of the shooter with the House of Power, reading the tremolos and vibratos of people shying away from the gray-green cloaked Sureri.

The path started where Origon first glimpsed the shooter, gun to his shoulder. It cut across the crowd, the spikes of fear in the melody decreasing farther from the source. And then it vanished. Origon scratched his head, then let his crest resettle. Surely the shooter continued to cause confusion as he moved through the crowded amphitheater. But there was nothing.

"Ori!" The shout intruded on his surveying, and he lost the thread of the music. The Symphony flashed by, leaving him with no sense of the shooter's path. Origon frowned. If he wanted to track the path again, he'd have to find another way. He turned to Rilan.

"What is it?" he asked, annoyed.

Rilan jerked her head toward the capsule, where the crew were scuttling toward the safety of the entrance. Origon's eyes widened as the strident base chords intruded again from the Symphony of Power. Smoke drifted past the edge of the scaffold, burning his nose. The dense fuel the pilot light would activate was heating up. The pilot flames had been going too long in the chaos. Soon the real fuel would start to burn, disastrous without a majus to control it. He stroked his moustache, thinking.

"Can the pilot flames be shut off?" he asked, again in the Trader's Tongue. The older woman—probably the captain, from the many bands of color on the sleeves of her jumpsuit—shook her head vigorously. She was hunched against the rail, only paces from the hatch leading to the interior of the capsule.

"It was designed to burn fiercely for a short time, Majus, to provide a power source for Majus Teju to use. If the real fuel catches fire too soon, it will burn out in an explosion the size of this arena. Many will be injured, and it will be multiple cycles before we can amass this much fuel again. Our flight to Ksupara will be scrapped. Can you direct the pilot flame? Could you fly the ship in Majus Teju's stead?" The woman must have been informed of his abilities.

"We're losing him, Ori!" Rilan called. She had her hands pushed tight against Teju, whose head fell back against the railing as if it were too heavy for him. The crew's doctor was trying to investigate the wound as she held pressure, but his hands were already soaked with blood, his doctor's bag next to him splayed open to reveal a variety of tools. "Even if we get him down from here in time, I don't think Doctor Chitra can save him.

There's too much damage." Her eyes were wet when she stared up at him. "Ori, help me make my people proud. I don't want this day to be a complete failure."

Origon looked to the dying Teju, to the burning smoke, the crew on the shaky walkway, and to where the shooter had disappeared, far down in the crowd. Who had gone against the trading might of Methiem? Who had disobeyed the wishes of the Great Assembly of the ten species, and the Council of the Maji? Both organizations had given approval to this endeavor. Without a culprit, there was as much chance of sabotage if the Methiemum tried a second time. But if they were able to get to their moon this day, he could do Teju's job: create a portal back to the Methiemum homeworld. Once complete, the knowledge could be disseminated, and travel to Ksupara could be an everyday occurrence, protected by the maji. And from there, farther into Metheim's solar system.

If he did this, he would be the one to guide the capsule into the sky, remembered as the first majus to fly a space shuttle.

There was really only one choice.

Origon pushed up from his crouch on the walkway, running to the capsule's entrance, ears straining for the sound of another bullet whizzing past. None came. The crew followed. One of the crewwomen began closing the heavy door of the capsule behind them and through it, he saw Rilan dragging the body of Teju back toward the ladder. The doctor was shaking his head, wiping blood from his hands and packing up his bag. Origon could investigate the body when he got back, assuming he got back intact.

Origon stepped through the short hallway to let the doctor pass, then followed the crew to the one circular room at the nose of the shuttle. He reached out with all his senses.

I shall be the one to put this capsule on Ksupara! The thrill raced through him. *The first time members of the ten species are traveling in space!* There would be time to grieve for a fallen majus later, after he returned from the moon. Honor and ceremony would accompany the return, though he pushed the thought away. *For now, it is critical to concentrate on the task.*

Around him, the eight crewmembers scurried to various tasks, flipping levers and tallying up sums on chalkboards. Several checked gauges for liquids coursing along walls of the room and down into the bowels of the lengthy cylinder beneath them. Origon stood near a half-sphere of metal, detailed with ornamental filigree, thrusting up through the center of the domed room. The burnished ceiling missed his topfeathers by a handsbreadth, and the diameter was maybe four times its height. Polished riveted walls reflected the light of Methiem's morning sun through small portholes filled with thick lead glass.

Origon ignored the scurrying Methiemum, feeling the awe inspiring verses of the Symphony of Power below him, like a thousand trumpets blowing at full volume. His mind recoiled from the roiling furnace of fuel attached to the bottom of the capsule. Surely this was too much? Once that melody was released to its full potential, it would consume the shuttle. But the Methiemum would not have designed it so poorly. He traced the racing lines of music describing the pilot flames, a candle to the sleeping sun in the tanks of fuel at the bottom of the shuttle. He could hear the shape of it in the languid Symphony of Communication. Air passed beneath it, blown through a tube by a slight breeze from outside. A small valve stuck closed, but a directed staccato trill, a burst of air, would be enough to switch the valve and let the pilot flame in. It would happen anyway, if he didn't control the burning pilot light first. It was designed for a majus to use.

"Is everyone to be ready?" he asked. There was little time before the pilot flame reached the main tank. Crew scurried around his unfocused eyes, and someone tugged on the sleeve of his robe.

"Please, sit, and tuck in your restraint," said the captain. Origon looked around. Everyone else was seated in reclining chairs around the periphery of the room, each stationed near a bank of dials and levers. They watched, eyes wide, firmly strapped in place. The captain pointed to one of two empty seats.

Origon sat, and the captain helped him buckle his restraints. His height made the seat uncomfortable—it had been designed for one of average Methiemum stature.

"Is this all to be necessary?" he complained.

"Quite so," the captain answered. "There. Done." She stepped back. "Please wait until I have restrained myself, and then feel free to start our journey, honorable Kirian." Quickly, the captain strapped in, then nodded to Origon. "Our lives will be in your hands."

He realized the captain and crew were terrified to have him here, rather than Teju. He assumed the younger majus had trained with them. Well, Origon had many more cycles of experience using the Symphonies of Communication and Power. There was really no need to worry. They would all be back by dinner.

He relaxed, letting himself float back into full absorption of the Symphony, feeling the chords surrounding him. The two Symphonies were separate, yet connected. Most maji only heard one sixth of the full music of the universe, but he was fortunate enough to be able to hear two Symphonies—one third. Each expanded in his mind from a single chord to individual symphonies to fractal themes swirling within each other, defining the interconnected phrases of Power and the multi-layered themes of Communication.

The capsule faded into the background. He found the catch again, air swirling around it, the opening for almost unlimited potential power. He sensed the tempo of potential and force with the House of Power, saw the restraints that would direct the liquid fire. Yes, that would most certainly lift the ship. He took a deep breath, changed one gracenote in the Symphony of Communication with his song, and flipped the valve open.

He was pushed back into his seat, neck straining to hold his head up.

Fire surged, more than he could bear. The tempo was a military drummer beating to quadruple time. Notes slipped through his mental grasp, far too fast to handle, much less change. He clawed through both melodies at once. This was the reason he was here, for Communication and Power had merged into one; burning air and a hurricane of fire.

The capsule was rising into the air, gaining speed, listing. Soon, it would veer to one side and then back down to the ground, digging a hole and smashing him and the crew into a paste.

The air outside the ship. He listened to that comparably languid music, felt the way the ship moved. If he could redirect where the burning air went, he could propel the ship the other way.

Notes slid by him, too fast to change, and he had the sensation of hanging. They were moving sideways. The crew might have been shouting, but he could afford no concentration for his physical ears. There *was* a pattern to the relentless beat of the fuel. He didn't have to catch the notes to change them. He instead saw their pattern, made the new musical phrase, crafted from his own song, ready to insert it...*there.*

The ship righted abruptly, but Origon felt his invested song ripped out of his grip, flying out far beneath them. The ship began to list to the other side.

Gasping, his stomach threatening to jump out of his throat, he realized what he should have before. He no longer envied Teju his place here. There was no chance to reverse any of the changes he made. Every change to the Symphonies on this trip would be permanent. The shuttle was flying so fast that the surrounding music was in constant flux, notes changing. It would strip each application of his song from his being. If he was not efficient, the flight would drain him to something insubstantial, his song stripped of its notes.

His body hung to one side and Origon made another construction from his music, inserting it into the breakneck beat, wincing as a small portion of his essence was lost. This could only buy time.

The flight would be several hours long. Ksupara was small and near to Methiem, compared to moons of other species' homeworlds, but would serve as a gateway to extensive exploration of the Methiemum system. He would have asked for chalkboard and chalk to make notes, but he could not move under such pressure. This would be by instinct and experience, guiding the ship the smallest amount while keeping to the most efficient path to space. How much *had* Teju trained for this?

He listened for the outer cadenzas of the Symphony of Communication, hearing the air currents far up into the atmosphere above the capsule. Below the tank of fuel, swirls of power and force made the music too discordant to follow. While his mind rode the vibrations of the air currents, planning their course, he wondered if Teju *would* have been able to handle this job, no matter the training. It was nearly beyond even Origon's grasp. The ship listed again, and he redirected the flow of the fuel with another change, a bit of his song thrust into the Symphony at the right instant. He felt weaker already.

For a small eternity, Origon molded the Symphonies around him, sweat dripping from his brow. His pointed teeth ground together with each jarring rip as his song disappeared into the air. Time flew by almost unnoticed as he put his full concentration into fighting his way through the air, a small sun strapped to his back. He *was* the capsule. They were moving fast enough that each change to Symphony was distant from the last. It was oddly liberating to repeat the same composition again and again. Yet every time he did so, the song defining him became more a skeleton than a sonata.

At some point, the acceleration lessened, and his arms began to rise on their own. His robe billowed out like a multi-hued balloon. Sounds—aside from the internal music of the Symphony—intruded on him, like one or more of the crew being violently sick. He would never shame himself like that. He stifled a burp.

The melody of the tank of fuel was lethargic now, nearly empty, and he had little need to use his song to effect changes. Origon opened his eyes, blinked, and licked his thin lips, realizing he had not moved or spoken for—how long?

"What is—" He stopped at his croaking voice and swallowed. The captain twisted fluidly in his direction, no longer pressed down by the great weight of acceleration. A lock of her long gray hair had come free from its bun, drifting like a halo around her head. She was highlighted by shielded carbon arc lamps, throwing great swaths of harsh light around the cabin. A chemical heater protruded from the center instrument cluster, warming the cold interior. Engineers must have installed the newer lights rather than relying on candles—too hazardous in space—or energy stored by a majus of the House of Potential. The crew fiddled with switches near them. Some had small lanterns to see detail by.

He tried again. "What is the time?"

"We've been traveling for nearly five and a half hours, honored Kirian," the captain said. "We were worried when you did not answer our calls, but our capsule did not falter after the first few minutes, so we assumed you were busy in your work."

Had they called to him? He searched his memory, but could not remember. "I am named Origon Cyrysi, Captain. What is to be done when the fuel tank is empty?"

"There is a way to detach it with your magic, Majus Cyrysi," she answered. "If all has gone well, you can begin our deceleration with the secondary tank. The hardest part will be landing."

Origon didn't bother to correct the woman's use of 'magic.' He was too tired, and even a few maji thought what they did was supernatural, not a science. He bent his head in concentration, seeking through the Symphony for the mechanism the captain spoke of.

There. Four large catches on the side of the empty fuel tank. Origon could feel the latent power, a slow steady beat, behind the explosive bolts. With another wince, he changed their tune in the Symphony of Power, building the melody to a snappy crescendo with his song. The bolts exploded and the empty fuel tank sliced away behind them, no longer on their trajectory. Of course the change was not reversible. The explosion disintegrated the bolts and the music describing them.

He knew the Methiemum built this capsule by menial methods, but had the designers not consulted a majus on how to control it in flight? Every little thing seemed planned to use up his potential. It would be a simple thing to modify the architecture.

Origon sighed. When he got back, he would track down the designers and have a long talk with them. The melody of Communication and Power between the crew—the little solos and trills that manifested in their body language—told him they were over their terror and growing more efficient at their jobs.

In the depths of the Symphony, there was a glimmer of a building theme so strident it would overpower the rest when it was louder: Ksupara itself. The House of Communication was weaker here, as there was little air, but the capsule was sealed well. He added his own cadenza to the melody of the air in the capsule, freshening it. That at least was not permanent. He retracted his song and the breeze died down.

The strident theme was getting louder. "Captain," Origon said. "Is there a way to be viewing our destination?"

"Certainly, Majus Cyrysi," the captain answered. She pressed a button and a section of metal slid aside, revealing thick glass. A neat piece of engineering. Through it, he saw a milky glow beneath them—Methiem. Above, a deep swath of black extended in every direction, sprinkled with tiny points of light. Several of the crew gasped, and his breath caught in his throat.

Shivers ran up his arms as he fixed the picture in his mind. He would remember it for the rest of his life.

Wisps of clouds raced below. Ahead, an irregular round object shone, reflecting light from Methiem. It had to be Ksupara. One of the other moons rose behind it, larger, and farther away. But the rocky surface of Ksupara was closer than it should be. Origon said nothing. No sense panicking the crew.

"That will help immensely," he told the captain, who nodded back.

Origon focused on the shining object and the heavy, rising theme which would direct their course. He would have to land the capsule, or rather crash it with everyone intact. The capsule did not need to fly back to Methiem. Those who came through later portals could hack it up for scrap for all he cared. He no longer had any interest in the fine design of the capsule. He let one shaky hand float up, imagining he might be able to see *through* his hand if he spent any more of his song. But he wasn't done yet. He took a deep breath in through his nose, resettled his crest, and blew the air out.

The Symphony of Power outlined the secondary tank, trills of blocked power humming. The tank had exit ports on all sides of the capsule, controlled by small nozzles, each with a lightweight valve. Once the fuel passed the nozzle, it would catch fire and push the capsule in the opposite direction. It was simple in principle.

There was only one problem.

Origon raised his head to scowl at the captain. "Did your engineers consult at *any* point with one of the maji?" he asked. She visibly paled under his gaze.

"We did, Majus. Is there a problem?"

Origon waved a hand irritably. "Never you mind. I will be addressing the problem myself."

The subtle vibrations making up the universe could only be pulled and changed so far and for so long. Once he grasped control of the valves to make adjustments, he could not let his focus lag from any of them, lest he could not move them a second time. He would have to maintain a focus on—how many were there?—*eight* separate valves all at the same time! Teju would never have held the capsule together. He wasn't sure *he* could handle it, and he had been out of apprenticeship for forty cycles, not newly raised from apprentice.

Origon sighed noisily, and the captain raised her eyebrows at him. The other crew watched too, but Origon ignored them. Their calculations and buttons did not regrow his song. Why hadn't the Methiemum designed a lever for *this* job? Eight people could pull levers, guided by a majus for the correct timing. By the great winged ones' beards, he would personally rend the designers of this capsule when he got back. *If* he got back.

"I wish for absolutely no one to disturb me until this capsule is resting upon Ksupara," he commanded. He glared around the room. "The less noise the better." Without waiting for a confirmation, he tightened his straps and clasped his long-fingered hands together, concentrating. He heard a chorus of fabric-on-fabric sounds as the crew followed his example, then silence. Origon stared out of the glass at the approaching moon, listening.

With the House of Communication, he could control the eight valves. Only a glissando was required to turn them on or off, but the notes wavered as if he heard them underwater, and he slumped in his chair. He found the first valve, clutched at the notes. Then the second, and the third. His breathing became ragged. Four. Five. He shook, just a little, then reached out and grasped the notes controlling the last three valves. The Symphony buffeted him, as the capsule sped ever nearer Ksupara.

He had to keep a connection to each valve to adjust any one of them in time. If he lost the connections, he would not be able to get them back.

Their speed was the first problem, and he invested his song in three valves pointing the direction they were traveling. His hands clenched at his chair's arms as liquid fire rushed past the valves, randomizing the air currents. Sweat popped out all over his body. But the ship slowed.

It skewed off course the other way. Ready this time, Origon opened two different valves and closed the first three, correcting.

Decelerate. Correct. Stop the twist. Sweat. Breathe. More deceleration. Repeat.

Ksupara was massive in the front view, and he ignored the captain's plaintive stare. They were going too fast. He wished he could close his eyes as he did for the flight into space, but he needed to see the moon through the glass. That meant more distraction from the crew's twitches and scared faces.

Decelerate. More. More. They were going into a twist, but he couldn't correct it at the same time and stay conscious. Some loose object whirled about the capsule. All the force must go forward to stop their movement. Another crew member was sick, and Origon fought down his own gullet. He closed two valves, opened two others. He had counted on more help from the air itself, resisting their movement, but had miscalculated. Not many realized how much air weighed, and the medium of communication here was much thinner than he expected.

With the small bit of rational thought left to him, Origon considered his options. Overshoot and they might never land. Crash directly down and they would most certainly die. What else was left? What could resist their movement? He watched Ksupara's ground coming closer at startling speed. From here, he could see valleys, short, eroded mountains, and large flat plains.

The surface itself. The insight put a pointy smile on Origon's face, making the captain's whiten in response. He ignored her and gently aimed the capsule just below the horizon.

"Prepare yourselves," he told the capsule in general. He heard rustling.

The impact jolted through him, his head bending forward, and his chair rattled in its bolts. He felt one of the valves crush, its music ceasing. It was a relief to hold only seven. He eased the capsule up from the surface, but there was a persistent vibration that shook his bones. A range of hills sprang up as they soared over the landscape and Origon gritted his teeth, opening all the valves on the right side of the craft. They veered left. The capsule trembled and twisted as one corner brushed the side of the highest hill.

Still not slow enough. Origon aimed the capsule down at a plain dotted with circular marks, keeping the forward valves open.

The capsule bounced off the plain, the impact shaking his chair like a leaf. Something bent with a screech that made his ears hurt. He rocked back and forth, lighter than he should be, as he readjusted their flight upwards to clear a hill. The ship was slowing.

One last time he touched the capsule to the surface of Ksupara, smashing another three valves. He heard the captain grunt. Then there was a crash from his left and a form flew across his vision. His was not the only loose chair. He did not have time or attention to spare for the occupant.

The capsule plowed through the dusty ground of the moon, cutting a groove. He could see a huge valley coming up fast, many times deeper than the capsule was tall. They were rotating sickeningly, and Origon felt for the correct orientation of the remaining valves. Waiting, waiting.

Now. He opened all of them and the ship rose, listing to the left. The valley sped by underneath them, reaching far into the moon. Someone screamed.

The reserve of fuel was nearly depleted—most of it had gone to decelerate the capsule. He could force them to the ground a final time, using the still intact valves now on the upper side of the capsule, but they would not rise again. He strained to see the edge of the valley, which seemed to take up half of Ksupara. Finally the far edge came into view—thankfully a plain, and not a mountain. Origon hoped he had cut enough speed to keep them all from dying.

"This is it!" he cried, and let the last remaining fuel guide them forward and down.

PART TWO

Violation of Natural Law

- The exploration of the sky above our worlds is a journey we will eventually take. Though ten species at least have found the Nether on their own, we are separated physically by uncharted distances. Certainly there may be other neighbors, closer. If we were able to explore the sky, might we find others and bring them knowledge of the Nether?

From the first Methiemum proposal to the Great Assembly on the subject of space flight

Origon awoke to a flickering light. It was a store-fire lamp, an artifact of the House of Potential, storing the song of fire from a majus of the House of Power. It showed the captain's face, close to his. There was a large bruise on her cheek and her gray hair had fallen out of her bun, draping her face.

"Majus Cyrysi? Are you well?"

Origon blinked wetness out of his eyes—blood?—and mentally checked himself. There were points of pain all along his back and neck, and his shoulder seemed twisted, but nothing broken. He nodded slowly, narrowing his eyes at the pain in his head. He was sideways, and the captain was standing on the rounded wall of the capsule.

"Are we landed, then?" He barely remembered to use the Trader's Tongue.

"Yes, Majus, and the crew all accounted for. Dipara has a badly broken leg, but thankfully nothing worse, for all she flew across the length of the capsule." Origon looked to the other side of the capsule at a sharp cry. A young woman was lying down, two other crew around her. He quickly averted his eyes from a shock of white protruding from her leg, glistening in the low light. "In addition, Doctor Chitra has suffered a concussion and is not able to ply his trade. Numerous other bumps and bruises among my crew. I will be speaking to the engineers on the condition of those seats when I get back." The captain folded her arms.

"You will wait for me to finish with them first," Origon told him, rubbing his neck. "I may not be leaving anything to complain to. Help me out."

The captain undid his restraints and Origon nearly fell from his chair, rolling in the light pull of Ksupara. He stood on the former wall and stretched, barely catching himself before he stretched straight into the air.

"Be careful," the captain warned. "You are far lighter on Ksupara. Lighter than on any homeworld—even Etan." Origon let out a short laugh. His arms and legs were barely able to hold him up, even here. If he had been standing on one of the homeworlds, he would have fallen over from fatigue.

Chairs and equipment hung sideways in the capsule, unlatched buckles dangling like hanging vines, casting shadows from the chemical lights on the center hub, now to his right at head level. One lamp was cracked and sputtering, but the others threw out harsh orange light. They had landed partially capsized, the flat bottom of the capsule in the air and the base of the rounded dome planted in the surface of the moon. The other side of the floor was now a peak far overhead.

Cabinets on the far side of the capsule hung open above them and Origon saw a jar fall out of them, curiously slow, to land next to one of the crew. Supplies were tossed about and underfoot and the crew was sep- arating them into piles, useful and not, broken and whole. The thick glass viewing window had not broken in the crash, though there was a crack running its length. It was vertical, now, the lower edge buried in gray-green dirt and the upper portion higher than Origon's topfeathers.

"Well, captain," he said, slumping back against his horizontal chair, "what is to be the plan? Are we ready to go back to Methiem? I believe I may be managing a portal, if you are giving me some few minutes to build up my strength." He could barely hear the Symphony. He had used up more of his song in the flight than ever before. He knew he should be angrier at what the cap- sule designers did to him, but was too tired to summon the emotion. His crest sagged in exhaustion.

"Oh no," the captain replied, sounding scandalized. She brushed her hair back, trying to make it lie straight in the light pull of the moon. "We will be the first inhab- itants of the colony on Ksupara. All supplies are included to turn this capsule into our base of operation. The plan," she looked around sadly at the ruins of her upturned capsule, "was to have the station function as it landed, but since things did not go, ah, quite as ex- pected," she gave Origon an apologetic half-grin, "we will make due. The tanks of air are planned to last us two days, though my mechanic tells me one developed a leak in the...landing. Likely we will have a day or so be- fore they will need to be recharged by a majus."

"One of the House of Communication," Origon add- ed automatically. They were the only ones who had the ability to achieve such a task. The captain looked con- fused and Origon dispelled his words with a wave of his hand. "It is not mattering. I will be leaving shortly, so anyone wishing to come back to Methiem should accompany me."

"Dipara will have to go with you, of course," the captain said. "And probably the doctor. The rest of us will stay here, and hope a replacement physician can come up with the next majus."

"Fine," Origon told her. He looked around at the crew. There was another cry as a crew member set the unfortunate Dipara's broken bone. He recalled he didn't know any of the other crews' names, nor that of the captain. He was more interested in getting back to Kashidur City, and seeing the look on Rilan's face. And taking a nap. His eyes were ready to close as he stood, and his breathing was labored, as if he couldn't pull enough oxygen into his chest. He listened to the Symphony, intending to use his song to refresh the stale air, but the music flashed by faster than he could concentrate. The beat was indecipherable. He flailed at the notes, and they slipped away from him as if greased.

He walked slowly across the curved side of the capsule, hoping the movement would refresh him. The thought of Kashidur City reminded him of the cloaked figure, running through the crowd. The assassin—the reason he was here. He hoped Rilan had uncovered more evidence. Maybe enough to capture the assassin himself when he returned to Methiem. He stood a little straighter, his crest righting itself. His eye caught the featureless plain through the window, a rounded mountain rising in the distance.

But to pluck another feather, how many days of one's life were spent standing on the surface of a moon? He stroked his moustache. It was the first space exploration of any of the ten species. And he was the first majus in space. There was time to revel it his accomplishment.

He stumbled the rest of the way toward the viewport, his feet bouncing off the floor with every step, skirting a pile of salvaged supplies fallen from the cabinets. His long and colorful robe, not as handy here as on the surface of a homeworld, swirled around his legs as he moved, showing a nearly indecent amount of ankle. He pushed it down, but the robe caught something and nearly sent him tumbling into the banks of controls. He grasped at a panel in a clatter of supplies, glaring around, daring the crew to comment. Most looked quickly back to their work. An urn of some sort clattered out behind him with a heavy *crack*, but he ignored it, striding slightly too fast to the window, catching himself on the wall to stop his forward motion. He flashed another look at the crew, dutifully minding their business. They would watch him as soon as he looked away. If he had not been falling-down tired...

And why would someone want to bring that dreadful urn he tripped over? Perhaps it carried dried foodstuffs. He shook his head and peered out the newly vertical viewport.

The surface of Ksupara was bleak; uninteresting. It was gray rock, pitted with crevices, stretching to the slopes of the eroded mountain. Dust stirred up by their landing clouded his view, but he could glimpse the stars above, clearer here than on any homeworld. His father, an impossibly religious Kirian, always told him each star was the soul of an ancestor who had gone before. Origon never believed it until now. The pure glory of each dot of light was hypnotizing. The patterns of stars were far different from on Kiria. There was no Ploughman here, nor Philosopher, nor—

"Majus!"

Origon turned irritably to chasten the errant crewmember. He stopped short, mouth still open.

There was a dirty, uneven ball, like skin stretched around pus, floating higher than his head above the pile of supplies. It was directly over that ancestor's-cursed urn, broken in shards. Origon watched the ball slowly expanding, unaffected by Ksupara's light pull, though everything else in the capsule was.

The surface touched a bag, hanging by one strap from a chair bolted to the floor, and with a crackle of energy, the cloth disintegrated, pulled into the pale skin of the ball. Origon heard a gasp from someone, and realized he had pushed back against the window, trying to get as far away from the thing as possible. He forced his crest flat, forced his shoulders to unknot. The maji were always to be seen as calm in the face of the unexpected. He reached for the Symphony of either house by instinct, but it was still faint, like music played in a different room with the door closed. The notes were slippery and he ground his teeth as he tried to catch even one.

The growing ball intersected the chair next. There was a screech like metal being torn and the chair distorted, pulling like putty into a swirl around the thing.

"Holy Vish!" someone cried, and Origon pulled back, his eyes widening. There were tiny bits of leather and cloth floating on the ball's opaque surface. It did not move but for its slow expansion. It was as if the sphere was planted in the air, grown from the size of a child's rubber ball and inflated like a balloon. Now it was almost half the size of a man. The crew crowded toward the walls of the crashed capsule, trying to get as far away as possible. Origon shivered.

"What is it?" the captain called.

"I do not know," Origon called back, his voice thin in the chill air. He eyed the wall above where the chair had been. "But it may be eating through the capsule wall as easily as it did the chair." He had to contain it, stop the threat. He had to change the Symphony. Such a thing should not be a struggle.

He shook again, rubbing his fingers together. It had been cold inside the capsule from the very beginning, yet the heater in the center hub gave out warmth. Now it felt as if the air itself was freezing. A knife of cold sliced up his back and he turned to the window behind him to see ice crystals condensing on it, blocking the view of the moon's surface. They spread to the metal walls like spiderwebs.

"Can you stop it, Majus Cyrysi?"

What did the captain think he was doing? Origon gave only a grunt in return. His pointed teeth chattered violently and he bit his tongue. The shock of copper and cold gelled his thoughts and the Symphonies of his two houses grew in his mind.

Origon strained harder than at his test for majus, forty cycles ago. Harder than when he first heard the beautiful music of the universe. A single note rose up in his mind and he brought it to his attention. It fractured into a second note, then a trill, then exploded into a Symphony of its own. He slid down the icy window, concentrating, trying to separate Communication from Power. The Symphonies of the capsule sprang up, giving the musical equivalent of the crew's hushed words, the dead air in the capsule, the still fizzing remnants of fuel in the lines, the connections from the banks of switches and levers, the dimming chemical lights and dying heater.

Around the irregular ball there was discord. Notes frayed, veered off pitch, and became dissonant. It was the counterpoint to its slow consumption of the capsule.

Investing so much of his song into their flight made changing a single note an effort. He might recover his old potential eventually, but it would be many cycles. A person's song could eventually return to full strength, defined by their every moment in time. He pushed aside the thought. Complaining about it would not change what happened.

"I shall be shielding it from doing any more damage," he called out. One of the nearer crewmembers nodded nervously in agreement.

He adjusted as few notes as possible, a couple each in the Houses of Power and Communication, putting just a little of himself into the change. He would compress the air around the floating thing. It left him breathless, but at least those notes of his song could be reclaimed when he let the air decompress.

Only a few scholars and maji appreciated the weight of air, and even fewer appreciated it could be compressed hard as rock. Simple air, with the correct transfer of heat, could be a powerful shield or even a prison. He reached out, applying his change, and bright yellow and orange light burst forth around the ball in a cage, squeezing inward. The heat of the action melted ice on the walls. There were calls of appreciation from the crew, watching the physical effects of his change.

But when the color touched the ball, the crystal yellow and orange lattice, visible only to him or another majus, shattered and dissipated. The changes he crafted in the melody fluttered and tore as the hanging mass' discord shredded through the Symphony.

Origon staggered, slipped sideways, and felt bile in his throat as the ice climbed upward again. The captain called out wordlessly at the obvious failure. That part of his song was gone, sucked into the thing before him. He could ill afford it.

A hand caught his arm. "Majus, are you well?" Worry was all over the woman's face. "Where did this thing come from?"

Origon could not summon the will to speak for a moment. He gasped on thin air. Then: "I am fine. I must try again. And I do not know." He waved the crewmember off, but noted the Methiemum woman stood close, ready to catch him if he fell again. Several others inched closer, pressing around the circumference of the capsule to get to him while staying away from the mass. He did not complain. The effort was not worth it.

Each person's song—that portion that intersected the Symphonies of the universe—was connected to everything. There was nothing it could not touch. But the ball had eaten his changes to the melody. Impossible.

He grasped for the Symphony of Power, not attempting to change, but only listening, for anything to tell him what the sphere of destruction was. There was nothing. Origon blinked, slumped against the freezing window. There was never *nothing.* Music fractured and died as the ball ate the console attached to the wall of the capsule. But that music was the decaying energy of the objects. Inside the ball, there was no energy, no melody. This sphere did not exist, as far as the Symphony was concerned. It was a void in the universe. It took the energy around it, breaking it down, and...what? What could it do with the energy it took if there was nothing inside it? Energy could not be created or destroyed—that was fundamental.

Origon grasped for both houses, their harmonious fractal of Symphonies, blended perfectly with every particle of the universe. With his entire composition of his existence, he reached out toward this thing that violated natural law...and failed.

He could not touch it.

Origon, for the first time in many cycles, was truly afraid.

This thing was more important than the assassin and the landing on Ksupara together. How had it come here? Was it made by an intelligent species, or could it be natural to Ksupara? What if it grew forever, eating its way through the universe? He had to bring this information back to the Council of the Maji.

The crew was staring in horror. Several clutched together for warmth, and one might have fainted. Origon shivered again. The ice had nearly covered the viewing window and the chemical heater was sputtering, though it was not in the path of the void. It was as if...as if the void were draining energy from everything surrounding it.

"A Drain, that is what it is."

"A what, sir?" the woman next to him asked. She had her hand out again as if to catch him. He struggled upright.

"It is draining energy, so I shall call it a Drain," Origon said. He discovered the thing, so he should get to name it. It bore down overhead, filling a good quarter of the capsule and growing. Soon it would reach them. Or would it reach the wall first? Either way, the capsule was claustrophobic. He hunched down, seeing the crew doing the same.

"We must all be going," he called out. "This, this *Drain* will be destroying the capsule very soon. I am afraid none of you will be staying here to build a base on Ksupara." He hoped he could hold the notes still long enough to make a portal. Otherwise none of them would be going anywhere.

"Majus Cyrysi," the captain called, halfway across the circumference of the room. The woman looked frustrated, her voice plaintive. It was obvious there was nothing to be done. Origon held up a thin hand, forestalling her.

"Unless you are able to breathe the cold vacuum of space, and survive *that*," he pointed a finger upward at the swirling pale mass, still growing—a second chair disappeared with a screech and the captain winced, "you will go with me. I am unable to alter this Drain. It will be destroying the wall of the capsule in moments. You all must accompany me through a portal back to Methiem." He drew in a lungful of thin air. The anomaly above them must be eating the very atmosphere.

"But...can't you do anything?" another of the crew asked. He was a young Methiemum, barely more than a teenager. He trembled, but held his back straight under the looming menace. Good lad.

Origon shook his head. "This is to be a matter for the Council of the Maji." There were mutters from the crew. To non-maji, the Council, each member the head of a house, was almost a thing of fantasy.

The captain bowed her head, then looked around the remains of her capsule. She spoke in a carrying voice. "Take only essential items with you. Calculations, observations, and mathematical equations have the first priority. If we are scrapping this mission, then by Vish, we're going to know how to do it better next time."

A shudder ran through the capsule. The void—the Drain—had reached the wall, converting it to nonexistence. Origon pushed the woman next to him and she started moving. The rest of the crew bustled at the captain's orders. Origon aimed up-slope, to what had been the dome of the capsule, where there was slightly more room to make the portal. They ducked as they walked, the mass ahead reaching down for them.

The crew scrambled to gather supplies and notes, leaving the dead weight of rations and clothes. The captain was holding the concussed doctor up with one shoulder and three more of the crew hefted a tarp holding the prone Dipara.

A horrible whistle grew, like a giant teapot coming to a boil. Origon looked up at the mass of the Drain. It had breached the wall and air was escaping into vacuum. Then the whistling stopped suddenly, as the Drain plugged the hole, eating both hull and air. They had moments left.

Origon set his feet, closed his eyes and strained to hear the Symphony again. The single chord rose up, duplicated, and split into the Symphonies of Communication and Power. He fumbled for the notes he needed, almost falling with the effort. The female Methiemum—one of two not supporting the wounded— caught his shoulder and held him upright. He let her.

Portals—one way holes from here to there—were one of the first lessons every majus learned. Yet there was resistance here. The Drain was taking his energy. He grabbed the notes, like lifting lead weights, and forced the measures and phrases to alter, blending his song with the melodies of this place and of the portal ground on Methiem until they were the same melody.

Sluggishly, a pitch black hole swirled into existence, ringed with yellow and orange. It pressed against what had been the top of the capsule, as far away as Origon could get from the Drain. The portal was just large enough to admit his height, but he would have to turn sideways. For all his song in the portal, it should have been half again as high and wide enough for three. The room tilted before him, and he leaned heavily on the woman. He could not faint. Not yet. It would be the death of them all.

"Orderly through the portal!" the captain called. She was at the back of the clump of Methiemum.

"I must go through last," he slurred. "Move." The crewwoman left him and he fell hard against what used to be the dome of the capsule, a curved surface not quite a wall. It was crafted of finely burnished steel, worth more than many wealthy members of the ten species would see in a lifetime. He didn't know why that was important. He gasped for air.

The improvised stretcher with Dipara and the three who carried it went through first, turning awkwardly, then the two free crewmembers, holding bundles of supplies. The captain paused to survey her capsule sadly, a small pack slung over her shoulder, and Origon would have cursed her for the wasted effort if he could have. The Drain was not even two body lengths away. It must have eaten most of the far wall and the floor by now. Finally, the captain nodded to him, then pushed the doctor through in front of her. She disappeared through the portal. Origon's head turned slowly to the malevolent ball. There was only one feeble light left. So cold. So dark. The Drain buzzed in his mind, deconstructing the Symphony, threatening the portal—

His head turned, so slowly, back to the patch of blackness next to him, ringed with his colors. There was something he had to do. Reverse the change he made? Yes. He began to unknot the melding of this melody, his own, and the one at the portal grounds, but it felt like untying cobwebs with heavy mitts. His eyes drifted shut.

"No." The word was soft. He must have said it, for there was no one else here. He had to be on the *other* side of the portal. His shoulder slid along the steel, and he stumbled into the blackness. As he lost consciousness, he felt the portal come undone and his song flowed back into him.

* * *

"Ori."

Someone poked him and Origon sat up, the Symphony of the room springing into his head. The notes slipped away as he tried to craft a shield of air.

He realized who had called his name.

"Where am I?" he asked Rilan. She was still wearing the formal white dress she used for Council business. This close, he could see the olive green scrollwork highlighting its contours. She saw him looking and gave an ineffectual tug at the garment.

"Finally awake," she mumbled. Then, "I've managed to hold the questions off to let you rest, but they're getting insistent."

"How long have I been sleeping?" Origon smoothed back his crest, ran fingers down his moustache.

"Most of a day." Rilan crossed the room and pulled a window shade open. Morning light from a sun still low made Origon wince. When they had left in the capsule it had been almost lunch the day before. When had he last eaten?

"One of the Mayoral Guard was waiting for you at the portal grounds. The crew shared their stories, and how you saved them. Ksupara is still there, so evidently a giant...ball...didn't destroy it. All their stories agree, or the mayor and the other officials wouldn't have believed them." Rilan frowned. "Also, Aditit's asking for you." She completed her summary as Origon pushed himself up from the bed. He hastily grabbed for his robe on a nearby chair and yanked it over his head. Not that Rilan hadn't seen it all before, but it was just indecent to show off so much arm and leg. He stuffed his feet into his boots, lying by the bed.

"Yes, yes. I will be going to her first," Origon said, and yawned. He still felt lightheaded, and hadn't had nearly enough sleep or food. The Symphonies of Communication and Power were still there, flowing through his head, but he dared not try to change the music. He pushed down a stab of fear at the thought of his song failing, and that he might never make a complex change again. He kept his face neutral. Rilan followed him out the door, to make sure he didn't fall over, he suspected.

"We're in the Mayoral Hall," Rilan told him as they exited the room. Origon looked around. A guard stood on either side of the door, one female, heavyset but muscular, the other male and skinny almost to unhealthiness. Both were dressed in suits, but he could see the bulk of leather armor underneath the cloth. They each had scimitars at their sides.

The hall was decorated in the prominent architectural style of the wealthy Kashidur province, tall fluted columns and glistening marble and quartz everywhere. Just as in the capsule, the Mayoral Hall was lit by carbon arc lamps, dim in the morning light. Normal bland Methiemum architecture. Could have used a splash of brighter colors.

Origon followed Rilan for a few steps, then looked back. "Why the guards?" No one would harm the hero of the first space flight. And they seemed familiar for some reason.

"The assassin," Rilan said, still walking. He could catch up to her easily with his long legs, so he watched the guards a moment. They looked steadily straight forward. He had almost forgotten about the assassin.

Something was bothering him about them, and he caught up to his old friend quickly. "Who are the guards answering to?" They made their way across the immense entry foyer of the Mayoral Hall, headed to a side room.

"Only the mayor," Rilan answered. "Nandara spared no expense in making sure the entire crew was protected when they returned. A couple are still in hospital, but the rest have retired to their homes, each with their own Mayoral Guard members to protect them." She threw a thumb over her shoulder. "One of these two was waiting at the portal for you." That explained the familiarity. "Old Nandara's a skinflint, but he's not taking any more chances with endangering his space-faring crew. He wants to show them off at all the award ceremonies Kashidur province will be holding. Can't do that if they're dead."

"He is to be a model of avuncular concern."

Rilan snorted. "You'll see."

Ten maji of the House of Communication were waiting for him in the side room, all Methiemum, of course. The species would have their own monopoly on traveling to their moon, at the start. Eventually, the location would get around to maji of other species, but the Methiemum might well construct a barrier by that point, to keep anyone with the location of the shuttle's landing spot from traveling farther into Methiemum space.

Origon nodded to Aditit Baska, a particularly old Methiemum female he had known socially for several decades, clothed in a boring dun colored dress. Her black hair had long since turned to a silvery gray, and her wrinkled and liverspotted face made her look more like a Kirian than a Methiemum. She and the others greeted him and Rilan politely. She was obviously the one in charge.

"Councilor. Thank you for retrieving Majus Cyrysi," Aditit said in her old, dry voice, then turned to him. "I'm glad you will finally share with us."

"I would have earlier, had I not left enough of my song in that ancestors-cursed capsule to nearly kill me," Origon told her. "I have been...recuperating since I returned. You must be cautious. There is to be a disturbance—a Drain—in the capsule. I am not knowing how big it is now, but I could not touch it. It had...it had no Symphony." He pulled on the end of his moustache, nervous. It pained him to even say that much.

Aditit pursed her lips. "This is hard to believe. I heard as much from the crew, though in layman's terms, of course."

"Of course," Origon agreed. They probably spouted off something about his magic being weak. Those who had not heard the Symphony did not understand.

"Astronomers have been searching Ksupara with their telescopes, but they cannot see the capsule, or its remains." Was that emphasis on the state of the landing? He wished Aditit had tried piloting that disgrace of a space ship. "They must take the word of the crew."

"The Drain will have emerged from a hole in the capsule," Origon said. It must have somehow stopped growing after they left, or it would be eating into the surface of Ksupara, surely visible by telescope.

"There is nothing," Majus Baska repeated. "Our scientists postulate it was an effect of the differing conditions on Ksupara."

Origon looked to Rilan, who shrugged. "I heard the same." A few of the maji in the background were whispering together, shaking heads.

He suddenly remembered the urn he tripped over, so out of place. The Drain appeared directly over it. Could it possibly have...? Certainly not. For that to happen would mean some person or agency knew about the launch, had resources to sabotage it, and had the means to create such an anomaly. Such a conspiracy would have attracted the attention of the Council of the Maji by now, if not the Great Assembly of Species itself. Better by far if it was a strange natural phenomenon. If they could only get near it again, protected this time, they could study it. Aditit and the gathered maji were watching him expectantly, and he frowned.

"I am not knowing what happened to it, but it was a Drain, I tell you. The Symphony did not touch it. I will show you, though there is to be danger in opening a portal." Once they could see the thing, their disbelief would vanish. Fortunately the House of Communication could bring their own air supply with them. Majus Baska nodded in agreement.

He stepped close, pressing his long fingers to the woman's temples, and felt through the Symphony of Communication. The notes were shaky. Origon took in a deep breath, letting the wash of music pass him by for an instant. Then he snatched at the phrases, barely catching hold of the notes defining this place. They would not slip away.

His rest must have refreshed him enough. Yellow light dripped from his fingertips as he summoned the memory of the surface of the moon: the dusty landscape, the musty smell of used air, the equipment laying helter-skelter in the capsule, the feel of being light as a bird, and lastly, the menace of the Drain. He rolled the melody over to Aditit, not making changes, simply using his song to show the way the music would be arranged to bring both sides into accord. It was a complex set of coordinates, half mathematical and half intuition. That was why it was left to the House of Communication to disperse the location of new portals to the maji population.

Origon stepped back, regaining the portion of his song he had used, and felt the room spin. Rilan's strong hand caught his arm, and he clutched at her to keep from falling. He heard a couple of the other maji gasp, and let go as soon as he could. Majus Baska was staring at him.

"The capsule took much from you, didn't it?" she said.

"I will be better in a few days," Origon lied. "I simply am needing sleep." He couldn't stand in front of the group of maji any longer, not in his state. "If you will excuse me, I am sure there are to be many more questions coming from the inquisition into the failure of the capsule. I hope to get more rest soon. Do not be forgetting the scarcity of the atmosphere on Ksupara." Once they saw and believed, then they could discuss the phenomenon of the Drain.

"Of course," the older woman said. Origon made for the exit in a hurry, trying not to lean on Rilan. The embarrassment.

He was almost to the door, Rilan surreptitiously supporting him, when Aditit called out, and Origon turned tiredly to see what else she required. The old Methiemum was staring ahead of her, brows wrinkled more than usual.

"It doesn't work," she said flatly.

"What?" Origon almost forgot his weariness. His crest surged upward in surprise. It wasn't possible. He had translated coordinates for close to forty cycles, in remote and unexplored regions. He did *not* translate them incorrectly. That was a mistake apprentices made, and not more than once. If a portal even opened with incorrect instructions, it might be anywhere. The complex mathematics involved were in no way linear, and a small change could result in a portal opening on the other side of the universe.

"Were you compensating for the difference in pressure?" he asked, more for words to say than anything else.

Aditit gave him a withering look. "I have been doing this since before you were born, Majus. I have opened portals to vacuum before. There is a reason I am the senior Methiemum in the House of Communication."

"Of course, Majus Baska," Origon said, placating, raising a tired hand. "It is not my intention to imply any disrespect." He was her equal in the House of Communication, even if she was the senior Methiemum. She was probably upset about the loss of Teju, as was he. "We have both been working with portals for many cycles."

He took a deep breath, and let it whistle out through his pointed teeth. He gauged the stress of opening another portal, while holding a pressure difference in the air around him. How much more of his song could he spare? But he owed it to these other maji to check his own portal. He knew the location was not incorrect.

He closed his eyes, but Rilan grabbed his elbow, swinging him around to face her. "Transfer the location to me," she whispered. "You can do that much, but Shiv desert me if you can do more without collapsing. I'm not letting you open a portal in your state."

Origon thought about arguing, and gave up. Rilan was far too stubborn, and furthermore, she was right. Rilan was House of Healing, so she could not change the air density, but the other maji in the room could easily hold the pressure difference at bay. He planted his feet to keep from swaying and grasped at the notes again. He was only showing how and where to make the portal, not actually making it. Otherwise the Symphony would not have let him do the same thing twice in such a short time. Wearily, he passed the location again, yellow light flaring, then leaned back against the wall to recover while she tried the portal. He was weaker than the newest apprentice.

Rilan had her eyes screwed shut, one hand out. No portal opened. A halo of white and green buzzed around her hand.

Her eyes snapped open. "It won't work," she said. "There's too much resistance."

Origon considered, following to the one possible conclusion. It must be the Drain. Ancestors only knew what the landscape looked like on Ksupara after the Drain stopped eating. His coordinates, what he experienced, was no longer accurate.

Once before, many cycles ago, an earthquake marred a portal ground on Kiria, plunging half of it underground. He had traveled there over land to re-establish the melody of the place for the maji. The Symphony was forgiving, with respect to portals. Rain would fall, plants would grow, air and earth would move slightly. Still the portals opened. The only way they would not was if the location of the portal changed beyond recognition. The capsule must be completely destroyed. And that meant any evidence of the urn was destroyed as well. He would have to start investigating it somehow else. At a later time.

He explained his thoughts, leaving out any mention of the urn. That would be his private investigation.

Aditit *humphed* after he was finished. "Unlikely," she

said. "But possible. Still, I trust your skill enough to know you would hardly give us the wrong coordinates. I must take this to Councilor Freshta."

Rilan raised an eyebrow. Origon knew she was sick of other councilmembers pushing her to the sidelines. If it had spread to the maji population as well...

"*I* will take this to the entire Council, not simply the head of the House of Communication," she said. "Unless you've forgotten my own place on the Council."

"No offense meant, dear," Aditit told Rilan. Origon could see his friend's back stiffen through the white dress. "Of course you should take this to the Council."

"I will come with you," Origon said hastily. It was his discovery—he should get the credit for it.

"After we meet with the mayor and the city elders, of course," Rilan said.

He grimaced. "Of course."

Aditit tapped her fingers together. "Then I will work here on Methiem. I have many tempers to soothe." She turned to the group of maji around her, assigning orders.

* * *

Origon watched the room full of well-dressed Methiemum dignitaries, bankers, and politicians. They watched him back; a sea of gray and black. They had been in the midst of a vigorous discussion when he and Rilan entered. Fortunately, they stopped so he could address them. He smoothed down the bright orange and yellow striped fabric of his robe, picking small bits of dust out of the blue scrollwork. The other species never had enough color in their clothes. He was standing next to Rilan at the center of a vast crescent of bench seats, occupying most of the area of the Mayoral debate chamber. Hanging scrolls and banners glittered with gold and red, and the walls shone white in the morning sun through a line of windows.

The Methiemum were primarily traders, and Origon gathered many had wagered significant amounts of their wealth on the success of the venture. No self-respecting Kirian would be caught dead gambling money on such a profound and philosophically important event as exploration of space.

"We heard you were taken ill after your voyage, Majus Cyrysi," a corpulent figure in the middle of the sea said. His voice was loud, used to public speaking. It was the same person who had "launched" the capsule—Mayor Nandara. "Still, Kashidur City owes you a large debt of gratitude. You seem much recovered. Maybe enough to give us your account?"

Origon glared at the assembled Methiemum, trying not to sway on his feet. The arrogance! "I am not much recovered at all," he countered, "as your capsule nearly killed me on the way to Ksupara. The design was to be so terrible it could only have been purpose-built to suck away the ability of a majus."

As he expected, the sea of gray and black began muttering and gesturing to each other. He looked to Rilan, who had a long-suffering expression on her face.

"You could at least try to make this easier instead of harder, Ori," she said. The noise of the room was enough that no one else would be able to hear her. He ignored her, waiting until the clamor died down.

"At least your noble sacrifice results in a new state of affairs for the Methiemum, and indeed for all species of the Great Assembly," Mayor Nandara said. It was all political bluster. Origon gave the room his best toothy smile—the one most Methiemum found disturbing. He did not like this mayor. Not that he liked many individuals who led power-hungry groups.

"Alas, I just discussed this with your Majus Baska. It seems the calamity which was to be endangering your crew is also preventing a portal to be made to Ksupara. You will have to commission another space capsule, I am afraid."

This time he heard Rilan sigh before the uproar swept away the sound. She leaned close to his ear. "This is why you don't get invited to share your new findings with the Council."

The mayor finally managed to intimidate the others into silence. "Our best majus," Origon raised an eyebrow at that, "was killed before he could even get in the capsule. We have heard reports it was one of the Sureriaj who killed him, perhaps simply an individual, but possibly with other interests behind him." Origon watched the sea of hungry faces closely. He had never seen the Methiemum as xenophobic, but as the sole alien in the room, he felt as if he was being judged, and found wanting. "The Sureriaj may be jealous of our technical abilities. Others may be as well. No offense meant to you, Majus Cyrysi, but you have seen the guards I must post to keep us safe. Isn't there any other magic you can do so we do not have to go through this effort again?"

"There is not," Origon told them, now wary. "The location was irretrievably lost. I, or some other majus, would have to again be walking on Ksupara. However, surely now the species have seen such a capsule can be built, they will be willing to help build another? You have paved the way for them." He didn't mention the Drain. That was a matter for the maji.

He looked around. Even Rilan beside him was quiet, her mouth pursed.

The mayor laughed—a stage laugh, meant to carry to others, but a laugh nonetheless. "The Sureriaj will not help us, as they have already sent one to stop us. Yes, there could be others of the ten species who wish to help, but as you yourself say, majus, none of your community would wish to pilot such a ship again."

"You may be correct," Origon said, but his mind was spinning. There was something wrong here—off. The mayor was making too many connections, too quick to point a finger at the Sureriaj. The emaciated face of the assassin popped into Origon's mind. The figure had been shooting at Teju. What had he thought at the time? The eyes. Could it even be possible? Was the mayor so corrupt? He barely kept his crest neutral. "And you must be excusing me now. New information has come up."

He ignored Rilan's grunt of surprise as he took hold of her arm and towed her from the chamber. The mayor's voice boomed behind him to stop, but he paid no attention. The guards at the door stepped in front of him, but Origon let Rilan's arm go long enough to grab at slippery notes defining the air currents in the room. The day was warm, and he took a little heat from all over the room with the House of Power, adjusting notes so that heat and air built a barrier between the guards and him. As he used his song to craft the change, he stumbled forward, spent, turning the movement into a headlong run from the room. He plowed into the wall across from the chamber, using it to change his direction as Rilan caught up to him.

"What are you doing?" she hissed, but he didn't answer. He reversed his change to the Symphony, sighing as his song flowed back to him and his strength grew slightly. He might be able to make it to his room without collapsing.

"Ori—what?" Origon stumbled on, up a spiral staircase, leaning heavily on the carved wooden bannister. "Shiv's kneecaps," he heard her mutter behind him, but she followed. He knew how to spin a mystery to keep her attention. He needed her for this.

Origon was breathing like a lathered cartbeast when he reached his room. He wouldn't even have been winded a few days ago. He was weak, and it was Nandara's fault.

The two guards were still there, and he gestured to them as he came closer, gasping before he was able to speak.

"It is to be...an emergency. Come...with me quickly." He opened the door, feeling the guards turn in behind him. Rilan must be in the rear. Perfect.

He reached his bed and turned, resisting the urge to fall into it. Indeed, the two guards were in front, Rilan in back. "Close the door," he told her, and she reached for the handle. Origon felt for the Symphony of both his houses, gauging if his song was strong enough to make the changes. He tried for the notes of the music of Communication, failed. He would be no help here.

But he could hear the connections between the two guards with the House of Power. They knew each other, comrades in arms, but there wasn't the close connection he associated with good friends or close family members. More evidence.

"Ori, what in the name of all the gods are you doing? You blew off the mayor of Kashidur, by Shiv's holy nose! I know you like to make sure you're in the middle of everyth—"

"Do you still trust me, Rilan?" he cut in.

"—ing." She stared at him a moment. "Yes."

"I am knowing where the assassin is." He carefully watched the guards as he spoke. They both reacted in surprise. The larger of the two only looked ready. The skinny one, the guard who must have starved himself to be that unhealthily thin, took a very slight step back, hand straying to his scimitar. Good.

Origon looked back to Rilan, straight in her eyes, then flicked his glance to the skinny guard. Back to her. "The assassin hid in the crowd because he was not to be Sureriaj. He was Methiemum."

He saw Rilan's eyes widen as she understood him, at the same moment the skinny guard drew his scimitar in a slice toward Origon's throat. Rilan, head of the House of Healing, youngest member of the Council, was even faster. One hand flew out, olive green and white flinging from it like droplets of water. Origon stood firm. He couldn't have dodged if he wanted to. Rilan's hand touched the guard's shoulder just as the scimitar connected with Origon's robe. The expression on the skinny guard's face changed from determined to pained as his arm gave out, dropping as if he had no control of it. The scimitar skimmed down Origon's robe and clattered to the floor at his feet. The guard followed, crumpling. Origon brushed away the wrinkle of fabric at his shoulder where the sword had started to cut.

"We still make a good team," he told Rilan. The other guard had her scimitar half out of its scabbard, but slowly eased it back in place with a metallic hiss, taking care to make sure both of her hands were in view. Origon nudged the limp body at his feet with one boot.

"This is one of the Mayoral Guard," Rilan told him. She looked to the larger one. "You wouldn't do anything without the mayor's approval, would you?"

The guard looked torn for a moment, her eyes taking in the body on the floor, then back up, mouth firm. "No, Majus. All the Mayoral Guard are of the highest character." She looked to the body again. "Almost all. He was a new hire."

Origon felt once again for the Symphonies of both Communication and Power. Observing the notes took much less strength than changing them. He could hear the connection between the two guards fading, notes of Power dwindling to piano, then silent. A whisper of the guard's last sentence still echoed very quietly in the music of Communication. The notes had the feeling of truth in them, the tones harmonious. Not a certainty by any means, but a good indication.

"Are you willing to be staying here and keeping your former associate from leaving?" he asked the guard. The woman nodded once, sharply.

"Good." He turned to Rilan. "I believe we are to be due a meeting with Mayor Nandara."

Rilan tugged her white dress straight. "I believe you are correct."

They found the debating chamber emptying of officials and representatives. Origon pushed through the flow, wishing he could spare a little of his song to force a path of air through them.

Mayor Nandara was there, talking to members of his cabinet. When he saw them coming, Nandara dismissed his advisors, who quickly exited the room.

"I see you finally made some time for me, Majus," the mayor said, disapproving. Origon felt his crest ruffling in annoyance.

"I have made time. Now I am finished with the assassin who killed Teju, I have plenty of time for you." The cabinet members were out of earshot by now, leaving the vast hall.

Mayor Nandara's heavy face drew down in a frown. "What do you mean?"

"I think you know," Rilan said. "The Mayoral Guard answers only to you."

"It does, but what does that have to do with anything?" Nandara pulled a handkerchief out and mopped at his receding hairline, where he was beginning to sweat. His other hand went to the small of his back, as if it ached.

"*Your* Mayoral Guard, that one who was dressing as a Sureri to hide, was just trying to kill me a few moments ago."

Nandara's eyebrows went up in surprise. "How awful! I shall be sure to investigate this shocking—"

"Stop it, Nandara," Rilan cut in. "We know it was you. I, a Council member, know it was you. What was the reason for sabotaging your own space program? Money? A rival?"

"Why, for Shiv's sake, would I sabotage—" the mayor started.

"You are knowing I am of the House of Communication, Mayor," Origon said. He spared a glance around. The room was empty but for them. "I can tell a lie when I see one." Not completely true, but the mayor didn't know that.

"I will be taking this to the Council," Rilan added. "I witnessed firsthand your guard attack Majus Cyrysi."

The mayor slumped, his heavy shoulders sagging. He wiped his forehead again, then stared off toward the door of the debate chamber, probably wondering if he could escape. Origon was about to add to their accusations when he finally spoke.

"You maji hold us back from progress. If it wasn't for you, we would already be traveling through space instead of through your portals."

"Yet I was to be the one to—" Origon began, but

Nandara cut him off with a swift motion of the handkerchief in one hand. The other came out from behind his back with a small pistol. Origon felt his crest rise in surprise. Rilan straightened.

"The maji are helpful in limited ways, but more often than not they are relics. Oh yes, stepping through a doorway of blackness to another place is easy, but you people also take away the challenges that force us to advance. Thirty cycles ago, I would never have thought to threaten one of you, let alone two. But with this," he motioned with the gun, making sure his arc covered the two of them, "I have the advantage in any negotiations."

"You can only take on one of us with that," Rilan gestured to the weapon with her chin. "You'll have to reload in between shots, and the maji will still have the advantage." She seemed calm, but Origon knew that was a mask over the furious storm raging in her.

"Wrong again," Nandara said, taking a small step forward, pressing them back. "Progress and new technology, remember? With this weapon I can fire up to five times without having to reload. Imagine how far through space we could travel, without you holding us back." Origon's mind raced to the assassination. There had been three shots in quick succession. More proof they were connected, as if he needed it.

"Now, let us proceed to this supposed assassin, and take care of the matter." Nandara waggled the gun for them to walk ahead of him.

The short walk up the stairs to Origon's room was nearly devoid of people. Now the meeting was over, the other members had scattered. A few servants ghosted through the corridors, but when one passed, Nandara stepped in, hiding the gun he used to push them onward. But not too close. The House of Healing functioned best by touch. Origon thought Rilan might still turn and grab the Mayor by his cravat, whatever the consequences.

The female guard was still there, watching over the skinny one, who was just regaining consciousness. The larger guard straightened to attention as she caught sight of the mayor.

Nandara shot her.

The gun was strangely silent, and Origon, shocked, absently noted the long cylinder attached to the muzzle. A dampener of some sort? Yes, the melody of the Symphony of Communication agreed with his assessment. The explosion's sound waves were not nearly as high in amplitude as they should be.

He watched, helpless, as the guard crumpled and the mayor turned the gun back on them. The guard fell as her former fellow rose to his feet.

"Forgive me sir," the assassin said to the mayor. "I was not able to take out the second majus, as you commanded."

"And see what a mess you have left," Nandara said. He gestured sharply to Rilan, who was creeping closer. Origon had hoped she would be able to affect the mayor on the way to the room, but no luck. He moved with her, close to the assassin.

"Kashidur province went practically bankrupt from funding the shuttle," the mayor said. "We had to make sure it paid back our investors in time."

"You would be getting many new minerals from space," Origon told him.

Nandara waved a fat hand—not his gun hand. "Too late, too late. The banking guild wanted real money, and soon. They've gone to adjust their accounts already. We had to guarantee the success of the mission."

"By shooting the majus in charge?" Rilan stepped

forward, but stopped as the gun's muzzle settled on her torso.

The mayor had a strange smile on his face. "Either success, or have the mission fail so utterly that it must be someone else's fault. No one was supposed to live to tell tales. It would have gone smoothly if this idiot hadn't messed up." Nandara nodded toward the assassin, whose face was slowly falling, as if he just now realized on which side of the gun he stood. "I could have gotten the Sureriaj back for that business a few cycles ago. We still have outbreaks of the Shudders, and a low birth rate in four cities."

"Shiv's spleen," Rilan swore, turning to Origon. "Ori, I *told* them you would be watching. That you were like Teju, but more experienced." She eyed the mayor. "And how did you know about the Sureriaj? It was supposed to be a secret."

Origon frowned at her. He had no idea what they were talking about. But the mayor ignored Rilan. "The Sureri assassin was an extra benefit. The design of the shuttle would show how the maji hold us back—"

"You egg-sucking son of a turtle." Origon glared at the mayor. Only his exhaustion kept him from changing the Symphony of Communication to squeeze this excuse for a person like a grape. That and he wasn't sure he was faster than the gun. "The shuttle was meant to be taking away my song. You were to be keeping me from interfering."

"And *he* was waiting for you, alone." Rilan flicked a finger to the assassin, next to her. "Ori, he would have killed you, weak as you were. And if he missed Teju, if Teju flew the capsule and returned, the guard would have been waiting for *him*, instead." She stabbed a glare at the mayor. "You have conspired to kill at least two maji. The Council *will* hear about this, Nandara."

The mayor raised an eyebrow. He wouldn't dare shoot a member of the Council of the Maji, would he? Better to distract.

"The only reason I was to be saved was the Drain," Origon said. "It threw a mallet into your works, did it not? The crew was not supposed to be coming through with me."

"A mess, as I said," Nandara told them. "I don't know where the damnable thing came from, but fortunately, you have found the assassin, who, in the resulting confusion, managed to shoot and kill two more maji before turning the gun on himself. Never fear, I can still set this all back on track and get rid of the interference of you maji."

"That is not—" was all Origon got out before the next shot took the assassin in the chest.

He grabbed the opportunity presented. He had recovered enough energy to control a gust of air. As the gun swiveled toward Rilan, it went farther than the mayor expected, pushed aside.

The rest was up to his friend's exceptional reflexes. Rilan saw the opening, as he knew she would, and lunged forward, knocking the mayor's arm aside, the bullet discharging with a *pop* into the wall of the room. The mayor's suddenly nerveless arm dropped the contraption and it clattered to the ground. A knuckle to his temple and Nandara dropped like a sack of grubs.

"I'm getting slow," Rilan complained. "Ten cycles ago, I would have disarmed him with no problem."

"Must be all the time sitting around with the Council," Origon observed innocently. "Dulls the reflexes." He bent to the assassin, who was gasping feebly. The man was choking words out—Origon heard whispers of it in the Symphony of Communication, but couldn't quite make it out.

"The holy...holy ves...vessel...made its...voyage." The light went out of the man's fevered eyes. Well, Origon was not one to judge others' beliefs.

"Now what?" He was exhausted.

"What in Shiv's holy earlobes was Nandara planning?" Rilan asked. "Keeping the maji out of the picture? Who does he think will open a portal to get to his new resources?"

"Taking the challenge out," Origon mused. "Rilan, do you suppose it is to be possible the maji do *too* much for others? By the ancestor's eggs. I was knowing the Methiemum were crafty, but this—"

"Why would they not want help from the Council and the maji?" Rilan countered. "The other species would jump ahead of us if we had to build a new shuttle every time we wanted to go into space."

"Unless the mayor planned to woo other species to be joining him in removing maji from space travel." Origon could almost, *almost*, see why. It was the same reason he traveled the homeworlds—the challenge of doing it himself. But surely not the right way to go about it.

"Whatever the reason, Nandara will not be so easy to take down, even with this evidence," Rilan told him. "His solicitors will argue this case before the Assembly and the Council of the Maji." Rilan growled. "*Idiot*. He could have done this cleanly. The Methiemum economy is already the biggest of the ten species. With the new minerals from space and the new trade agreements, it would have been unstoppable, and they would only have paid a few tariffs and fees to the maji to create a new series of portals. But now..." Rilan's expression promised retribution. "Even my own people must be held responsible for assassinating one of the maji. No amount of profit is worth it."

"This is not to be just the mayor's plan, is it?" Origon asked.

Rilan shook her head. "Sometimes I'm not proud to be a Methiemum. Believe me, they meant to do this, exactly this. They wanted a new source of wealth, but thought they could take the maji out of the equation at the same time, and even coerce other species to do the same." She shivered. "Maybe we are becoming outdated."

"Not completely. The Drain foiled their plan," Origon mused. "A positive result, for an object so destructive. Without a majus, the crew would never have escaped." He pounded one fist into his other hand. "I must be studying the phenomenon more. Where does it come from? Was there some catalyst on Ksupara?" He nudged the assassin's leg with a boot. "If only this 'holy vessel' had not made its voyage yet."

Rilan looked askance at him. "What's that supposed to mean?"

Origon shrugged. "His last words. I assumed it was one of your religions."

"Not one I know of." Rilan was silent a moment. "You don't suppose he meant—"

Origon looked down at the body. "The mayor as much as admitted the Drain was not to be his doing. But what if the assassin had other orders?" He ran his fingers down his moustache in thought. A holy vessel? Unholy, more like.

"Rilan," he began, "there is one more thing." He described the urn, and how out of place it seemed with the rest of the supplies. His old friend listened, her face tightening.

"The very act of creating this void in the Symphony keeps us from traveling to its location by portal," Rilan said. "As if the thing was designed to prevent maji from investigating it. Where did it come from? How do we study something like that?"

"We do not," Origon said. "Not until we return to Ksupara." He paused, as an awful thought occurred to him. Where *had* the urn come from?

"What is it?" Rilan must have seen his expression change.

"Or unless another Drain forms, elsewhere." Now her face mirrored the horror he felt.

"Vish preserve us, I hope not," Rilan said quietly. "Let this be an isolated event. Are you sure it was the urn that created the void?"

"Ah...no," Origon admitted. "It could have been a natural event, or perhaps it was to be a reaction to what was in the urn." No way to tell now, with the sole person who might have been connected lying dead at his feet.

"There will be a second capsule built, now it's proven possible." Rilan gestured vaguely with one hand, encompassing all of Methiem. "We will discover more evidence the next time we get to Ksupara."

"Then I am supposing we must include a majus on the flight," Origon told her. "Though it will not be me." He looked out the room's lone tall window. He could not see Ksupara in the day, but it was out there, waiting to be explored, as were the moons and solar systems of the other homeworlds. Even if the maji did not help, the ten species would go there eventually. And he would learn more about the Drain, one day.

"Then we must leave the mystery of your void for now, and hope there's no need to explore it further." Rilan grunted as she began to heave the corpulent mayor to a sitting position. "For now, we have to deal with him. Help me out. We'll bring him to the Council before he wakes and runs to his solicitors."

"Can you do that?" Origon tried to remember the councilor's powers in an emergency situation.

"I have some privileges, even if the other councilors ignore me as often as not. Come with me back to the Nether, Ori," Rilan told him. "We'll take the mayor and his plot to the Council now, today. And you could stay with me while you recuperate. It's been a long time since we had a real chance to talk, and your apartment is probably full of cobwebs and spiders."

"Too long," Origon agreed. "And what of the Drain? Shall we be discussing it with the Council as well?"

Rilan hesitated, holding the unconscious mayor's form up. "They'll learn of it," she said. "But maybe best not to press the issue for now. We have to hope this is an isolated incident."

Of course she was correct. Rilan's position with the Council was tenuous enough without wild stories about voids that lacked the Symphony. She had been busy on the Council while he had been traveling the home-worlds. He could aid her out now he was back. Origon helped her lift the mayor. They would alert others to the mess in the room, make sure none of Nandara's associates arranged the evidence against them. Origon would let his song regrow, and with that new music, discover what, or who, was behind the Drain.

Origon and Rilan will return in:
Seeds of Dissolution

ACKNOWLEDGEMENTS

The second book is easier than the first. Not the writing part, which is still hard. But once the publishing path has been paved the first time, the next is a little easier.

But there are many others who have helped me out. The first thanks always goes to Heather, for "letting" me do this, as well as for copy-editing. Second, a big thank you to my alpha and beta readers: Jeremiah Reinmiller, Courtney Brooks, Reese Hogan, Kaisa, Robin Duncan, Krystalynn, and Richard Pulfer. And thanks to all the folks at Reading Excuses for critiquing my submissions. Special thanks to Spieles for the orphans and throwing spice! Micah Epstein does awesome work and put together a great cover. Check out his paintings at micahepsteinart.tumblr.com. Also, thanks to Adam Riong for the interior art. Finally, many thanks to the members of the Writing Excuses podcast for spending their valuable time teaching and encouraging new writers.

ABOUT THE AUTHOR

I am a North Carolina native and a lifelong fan of science fiction and fantasy. In no particular order, I am a mechanical engineer, a karate instructor, a video and board gamer, a reader, and a writer. In my spare time, I wrangle three cats and one bald guinea pig, and my wife wrangles me (not an easy task). We both enjoy putting our pets in cute little costumes and then taking pictures of them repeatedly. You can visit me at williamctracy.com.

What's next? Stay tuned for Seeds of Dissolution, a full novel and the first of a series.

Please take a moment to review this book at your favorite retailer's website, Goodreads, or simply tell your friends!

Thanks for reading!
William C Tracy

86401951R00096

Made in the USA
Columbia, SC
14 January 2018